THE ADVENTURES OF CROC-MAN & WOLF-GIRL

First published in the UK in 2021.

ISBN: 979-8-72-834386-8

The Adventures of Croc-Man and Wolf-Girl: Rise of Dr.Fishnip

www.facebook.com/crocmanandwolfgirl

For Eloise and Emma.

And all the children who dare to dream.

INTRODUCTION

Dear Reader,

I would like to start this story by introducing you to Croc-Man and Wolf-Girl; a mutant crime-fighting duo who live within the vibrant and bustling Cruz City. Each day they keep the citizens safe from the many nefarious, crackpot villains that threaten to destroy the city on an overly regular basis.

Though they fight as a partnership, Croc-Man and Wolf-Girl are extremely different in many ways. Croc-Man, for example, has super strength and can lift a car with only one arm. Wolf-Girl, on the other hand, can hear things from many miles away and can run faster and jump further than anything else on the planet. Croc-Man and Wolf-Girl have not always had these abilities though, and soon you'll find out exactly how they became the legendary super-animals they are today.

Fighting evil in the crime-ridden city is an occupation that's quite new to them. Indeed, their lives were much more ordinary just a short while ago, prior to the strange events that would suddenly change their lives forever. In this origin story I'm about to share, they're going to come face to face with Dr. Fishnip, a part-fish, part-robot nemesis that dreams of ridding the earth of anyone and *anything* that doesn't have fins.

You read that right.

Dr. Fishnip *believes* that fish should rule the earth, and *he* should be their leader. But I'm getting ahead of myself...

I'd like to tell you a little more about Croc-Man and Wolf-Girl, because you're surely itching to find out how on earth a crocodile and a wolf teamed up to become the famous dynamic duo that are now loved the world over... I mean, that's why you're reading this book in the first place, right?

The incredible thing – *and this is extremely important* – is that I, the author of the book, have heard these stories first-hand.

Yes, I *know* Croc-Man and Wolf-Girl and they've person-ally shared all these stories with me. So, everything is true... from *their* perspective at least.

Anyway, let's get going with this frankly unbelievable story. Honestly, I've been brimming with excitement to be able to share this with everyone, so I'm glad you've chosen to enter this world, to get the full story on how two *very normal children* would accidentally go on to become *two very special superheroes*.

Yours sincerely,
Riley

1

WILLIAM AND VANESSA

William Walker was 13 years old and hated getting up for school in the morning.

It wasn't that he didn't like going to school *specifically*, he just *loved* to sleep for as long as he possibly could in his king-sized bed. It was simply the most comfortable thing in the world to him – like a big, soft, fluffy cloud that he could sink into and feel cuddled by.

He would lie there and listen to the birds outside, imagining he could understand the conversations they were having...

"You got much on today, Pigeon?"

"Not really, Robin. Might go into the farmer's field and get myself a nice juicy worm. Or maybe take a trip to the beach and see if the seagulls have left any chip scraps for me."

It was silly. He knew animals didn't really talk to each other like that, but it was something he used to do with his mother when he was very small, and it had become part of his morning routine now.

Another part of his morning routine tended to involve his dreadful stepmother, Hilda, who particularly delighted in creeping into William's room like some kind of spooky apparition, before swiftly dragging him out of bed.

She swore she was doing it for his benefit, to make sure he made it to class on time, but William knew that Hilda didn't really care much about his schooling, she just wanted him gone from the house.

In spite of his love for his bed, William *wasn't* a lazy child. In fact, he was in *all* the different sports teams at Foghorn High. He enjoyed football, hockey, rugby, rounders, basketball, cricket, tennis, swimming, gymnastics, running, badminton and tiddlywinks.

Some might argue tiddlywinks isn't a sport at all, but William took it very seriously and put a lot of extra effort into his training. Also, it was notably at an after-school tiddlywinks session that he first met his future best friend, Vanessa.

Vanessa Holness was also 13.

Or, 13 years old, 5 months and 20 days to be *exact*.

When given the opportunity (and even if people didn't ask), Vanessa had the unusual quirk of imparting incredibly specific information. For example, if you asked her the time she might say "it's three fifteen p.m., and 27 seconds". Or if you asked her how far it was to walk to the park, she might tell you it was "one point six zero nine three four kilometres". Depending on where you were stood at the time, obviously.

She also happened to be a fountain of (quite often useless) information and learning and reciting facts was one of her favourite pastimes...

"What year did Elizabeth II become Queen?"

"1952"

"How many countries are there in the world?"

"195"

"Who holds the record for the highest number of non-stop push-ups?"

"Charles Linster in 1965. 6,006."

She seemed to know *everything*. Or perhaps she was just very good at lying, because most of the time nobody ever bothered to fact-check. And though people tend to hate a resident smarty-pants, William found Vanessa to be a lot of fun and knew he'd never run out of unique things to talk to her about.

FOGHORN HIGH

The day that William and Vanessa first met started off like any other. Hilda had gripped both of William's pale skinny ankles and swiftly dragged him out of his cosy bed, bringing him crashing to the hard floor below.

"Ooof!" bellowed William, feeling the impact on his back.

Hilda even repeated the same boring line that William had to wake up to every day: "You've got school, you lazy toad. Get a blinkin' move on!" Her voice was shrill and would send a shivery wave through William's body.

However, William would *always* get to class on time, because through much practice he'd managed to get his morning wake-up routine down to a speedy 9 minutes, 35 seconds. That included breakfast, shower, teeth brushing, getting dressed, combing his hair, making his lunch, packing his bag, putting on his coat, then his shoes and finally tying his laces.

Hilda also had her own morning routine, and it took shockingly long for her to apply the copious amount of makeup she required (57 minutes, 29 seconds, last time William timed her). She would put so much on, that by the end of the day she could peel her makeup off like a snake shedding its skin. The thing was, William knew that whatever mask she tried to paint on her face, it was what was inside that counted. And what was inside was, quite frankly, dreadful.

* * *

Friday was William's best day of the week because Fridays meant Tiddlywinks Club. And at the end of this school day, where our story properly begins, William had found himself competing against the aforementioned Vanessa.

They were having an extremely close and intense game and a small crowd had gathered round their table to witness the excitement. The collective "oohs" and "aahs" echoed through the corridors at Foghorn High, with the audience gripped by the high level of skill on show.

Tiddlywinks appears simple, but it's extremely tactical, and it takes a great deal of practice to master the firing of winks with a squidger. A squidger of course, being the name given to the disc used to fire the other discs with.

After almost an hour of play, it would eventually take an absolutely masterful shot from William to settle the match. Vanessa rarely lost, and hated the feeling it gave her, but with William she knew she'd been beaten by one of the best players she'd ever come up against.

———

"Hey, you! Wait up!" bellowed Vanessa as she chased out the tall school gates after William, minutes after finishing their game.

"Oh, um... Hi..." said William, surprised by her sudden appearance and chirpy manner. Compared to the intensity and aggression Vanessa had shown during their match, it was like William was talking to another person entirely.

"You were rocking a *very* cool technique back there," said Vanessa, in a soft, well-spoken voice. "Great focus too. You were like a professional." Vanessa slung her heavy grey rucksack over her shoulder and began to walk beside William.

William could feel his face blushing and was hoping that Vanessa hadn't noticed. He wasn't used to getting compliments from girls, or really anyone for that matter, and nor did he know how he was supposed to reply.

"Yeah, um... Right, yeah. Um... Thanks, I guess?" William said, struggling for the right words. "I suppose I've practiced a lot. And... Um... And apparently practice makes perfect?"

"Yeah," agreed Vanessa, "I've heard that saying too actually. Personally, I used to play in a lot of county tournaments before I moved here. Yes sir! Many, many hours of repeatedly flicking plastic counters into cups. But don't get me wrong, it was super fun. Honestly though, I can't even begin to imagine how many hours I've put into this sport."

Vanessa was talking so fast that William wondered when she might find the time to breathe. However, she wasn't stopping just yet: "If you asked around, people would tell you I was one of the best players in our area, and I even got printed in the town paper. Lots of kids in school thought playing tiddlywinks was lame. They'd even tell me so to my face... Which I thought was totally mean, but I didn't really care because I enjoyed it, and if you enjoy something you shouldn't feel embarrassed about it. Right?"

William didn't mind Vanessa's chattiness, but was finding it hard to get a word in edgeways. He also found his attention drawn towards the large pink bow on her head, nested in her hair in a way that seemed to defy gravity.

"Sorry," Vanessa said, grinning, "I tend to talk a lot about myself when I meet new people. Dad says it's a bad habit."

"That's okay," William said with a kind smile. He was feeling a little more relaxed with her now, and words were becoming much easier for him to find. "I really enjoyed playing against you earlier. Honestly, it was nice to have a bit of competition for once."

They had been walking side by side for a few minutes now and had gotten completely lost in their conversation. So much so they hadn't realised that they'd crossed a busy road, walked through a small housing estate, taken a narrow passageway that ran by the side of the local grocery shop, and were now entering the park. And they continued to walk and talk for a good while longer, quickly learning that they shared a lot of similar interests.

Their friendship was truly forged as they talked about their favourite TV show (Teen Titans), their favourite 'vintage' band (The Beatles) and their favourite book (Harry Potter... all of them). In retrospect, it was simply crazy how alike they were, and after just 15 minutes of walking together, it felt like they'd known each other for years.

"Did you say you've recently moved here?" asked William, recalling something Vanessa had told him earlier. Vanessa nodded, and went on to tell him that she'd only just arrived in Cruz City due to her father's new job (which had such an unnecessarily long title that Vanessa couldn't recall it), and today was her first full day at Foghorn High.

"The school's pretty tiny though, isn't it?" said Vanessa. "My last school had 845 pupils, 42 staff members, 3 rabbits, 9 chickens, 4 guinea pigs and a chameleon."

William was impressed. After all, Foghorn High had only a fraction of that many pupils, only 10 teachers and absolutely no pets. Unless you counted Ratty the Rat, the resident rodent that would often be seen scurrying down the corridors.

The main school building at Foghorn High was tiny, exemplified by the fact it stood between two large multi-storey skyscrapers. From a distance, it looked almost like a doll's house in comparison.

That's if you could even see it, of course...

The school was easy to miss behind the many overgrown weeds and tall trees that stood in the courtyard. William had always thought that Foghorn High looked like it was trying to hide itself through embarrassment, but the truth was it had just been neglected, ever since the janitor had mysteriously disappeared a few years back. The Headmaster couldn't afford to replace him due to budget cuts, and so the outside appearance of the school had suffered in a big way. Sadly, Foghorn High was now simply falling apart at the seams.

The school hadn't always been so ramshackle though and had once been highly recognised for its basketball team, 'The Sharks'. In 1984, Foghorn High gained worldwide recognition when its team got to the All-Star Finals. The championship winning match had been televised across the country and had given the school a brief period of fame.

Even today, the school's Headmaster would often pull out an old video cassette and play the children highlights of the match in assembly, hoping to inspire them to be able to reach those heights once more. But without enough money to renovate the ancient gym hall and basketball courts, it was a total non-starter.

Truthfully, not one of the kids believed the school had any chance of that kind of success again, though that didn't stop William from dreaming of playing in the All-Star Final, *slam-dunking* the winning shot of the match... The crowd of kids would get to their feet, a roar of applause echoing out through the school hall, and William would be carried off into the sunset on the shoulders of his proud teammates.

W illiam had never felt particularly special. His dreadful stepmother, Hilda, would often tell him he was the most average person she'd ever met. He'd been told this so many times now, it almost felt like it *had* to be true, and that this was to be his one defining characteristic in life. Where other kids might be described as smart, pretty, sporty, or funny, if you looked up 'average' in the dictionary, there'd be a big picture of William. At least, that's what he thought. Still, it didn't stop William from dreaming about a better life. His imagination was always the place he would escape to, because in his mind he could be *whoever*, or *whatever* he wanted to be.

In fact, he was having his absolute favourite match-winning basketball daydream when he almost walked into a cyclist in the park. Vanessa saw the accident about to happen, and deftly shoulder-barged William to the side.

"Oi, watch it!" shouted the angry cyclist as he whizzed by.

As Vanessa turned around to look at William, proud of

her fast reactions, she immediately saw it hadn't quite been the heroic rescue she'd imagined.

"Yikes, what was that for?" groaned William as he removed himself from a hedge, clearly oblivious to the near-miss that had just taken place. He grimaced as sharp, pointy twigs scratched at his skin.

"Sorry," Vanessa replied, gritting her teeth in embarrassment. "Sometimes I forget my own strength... Although actually, you might not have realised it, but I sort of saved your life just now, because if I hadn't push..."

Vanessa cut herself off mid-sentence, noticing that William's attention had been stolen by a piece of rubbish on the tarmac path. Curious, William picked up what appeared to be a scrunched-up piece of paper, and slowly unfurled it.

His eyes lit up.

"Woah!"

Vanessa joined William and saw that he was clutching a vividly coloured poster. And printed on it was the image of a moustachioed man in a very fancy-looking tuxedo and bow tie. His face appeared to be bursting out the middle of the poster, and chunky black words surrounded him that read: "The Return of El Presto. Live on Stage!"

"Oh, I love, love, love El Presto," squealed Vanessa, grabbing the poster from William's hands.

"Me too," agreed William, snatching it straight back. "I used to watch his show *ExperiMENTALS* all the time. I'm probably his biggest fan."

"Hmmm... that's debatable," replied Vanessa, knowing that she'd seen El Presto's TV specials at least 236 times at last count. But at this point she didn't want to argue, considering she'd only just pushed her new friend into a prickly hedge, and he was still clearly feeling a little sore from the accident.

"Anyway, does this say he's coming to town?" said Vanessa, investigating the details of the multi-coloured artwork.

William's eyes opened wide when he saw a yellow banner stretched across the bottom of the poster, which read: 'Tickets Still Available'. They opened even wider when he saw the date of the next performance.

"Yeah, and I think he's performing a live show *tonight*?"

"No. Way... Really?" said Vanessa, barely believing their luck.

William quickly inspected his watch for today's date. Then, he compared it to the date printed on the poster. Vanessa was holding her breath in anticipation, until the second she saw a wide grin cross William's face.

"Vanessa... You're not going to believe it... That's today's date!"

Vanessa hopped up and down excitedly like an arcade Whack-a-Mole, and her habit of fast, breathless talking kicked in once again: "I want to go! Shall we go? How do we buy tickets? Can we get front seats? Is it expensive? Do you want to come with me? You do really want to go, right? I mean, I know we've only just met today, but please say yes! Please say yes!!!"

William looked at Vanessa, and his goofy smile told her everything she needed to know...

Yes. Tonight they would both be going to see the marvellous El Presto *live and in person*!

3

THE GREAT EL PRESTO

El Presto was mostly known for his TV show 'ExperiMENTALS' where he'd create and perform weird and wacky experiments with members of the public. His brand of 'science magic' had made him one of the most popular celebrities on the planet, because he'd made science *cool*. The things he did were unexplainable. Unbelievable!

One time on his TV show he helped an elderly lady named Edna Eddinbridge to realise her dream of shrinking down tiny enough to be able to ride on the back of Purrkins, her pet cat. On another occasion, he created a headset for a 10-year-old boy named Gordon Snufflebeam, which gave him the ability to become pixelated, like a real-life Minecraft character.

His most famous experiment, however, had been on a recent TV Special, when he gave his pet goldfish the ability to talk. El Presto poured a green oozy substance from a test-tube, directly into a fishbowl, and by the time the commercial break had been and gone, the goldfish had grown vocal cords.

The initial indicator that something amazing was happening was when a flurry of bubbles popped out of the fish's little mouth. El Presto quickly positioned a microphone in front of the fishbowl, hoping to pick up the first words ever spoken by an aquatic creature. But in the water, it was impossible to understand what the fish was trying to vocalise.

El Presto had planned for this event, though, and picked up a small net from nearby, positioning it carefully inside the bowl so he could catch the fish.

"He's a slippery little fella," said El Presto as he finally retrieved the goldfish from the cold water.

El Presto held the fish gently in the palm of his hand as it wriggled and flopped around.

It began to make the *strangest* of noises.

"Glup, glop, blurp, blip, bloop!"

To a human ear, the sounds were impossible to decipher. It just sounded like utter babbling nonsense. El Presto placed a strange contraption he'd labelled 'TRANSLOPEDIA 500' close by, flicked a switch, and after a brief flurry of beeps and whirrs, a high-pitched voice began to emanate from the speakers:

"Hey, put me back in the water, stupid magic-man! I can't breathe! Put me back or meet your doom *you pathetic human!"*

These were *indeed* the first words ever spoken by a fish. This was *indeed* a ground-breaking moment in history. And this was *indeed* a *very* angry little creature.

William remembered one surprising moment towards the end of that TV special, where the fish had almost sneaked out of El Presto's hand, nipping the magician on the thumb in the process. Fortunately, goldfish only have very tiny flat teeth in the back of their mouths, and so El Presto managed to easily slip the fish back into its bowl, foiling the escape attempt.

This experiment, which had been broadcast live to the entire world, was deemed a huge success for the magician, yet again proving he could *'make the impossible, possible'*. And it was those words which were emblazoned in BIG LETTERS across the back of the poster that William clutched in his hand.

"I'll get my mum to buy our tickets straight away," shouted Vanessa, as she began to sprint away towards the park's exit.

"Oh, um... Yeah, that would be *magic*. Thank you!" said William, trying to be funny. Though it was too late – Vanessa had already disappeared around the corner and was well out of sight.

William had never really had a best friend before. Well,

there was a kid called Henry Fletcher once upon a time, but William wasn't sure he'd ever genuinely liked him. Henry used to do this thing called 'belch-boxing' which was like beat-boxing but instead with burps.

At first William had thought it was quite amusing, but soon it became very annoying, and by the time their friendship had ended it was making him feel icky inside.

Eventually, Henry moved to a different school, though William had never found out exactly *why*... Some said he was caught stealing the Headmaster's chicken, egg and pickle sandwiches. Others suggested that Henry arrived at school one day on a stolen donkey, following a three-mile police chase through the busy streets of Cruz City. Whatever the cause, William didn't really care; he was just pleased to not have to smell any more of Henry's repulsively cheesy burps.

However Vanessa was certainly different. He'd only known her for a short while, but she was instantly fun to be around – the type of person that would laugh at your joke even though it wasn't funny. More importantly, she made William feel wanted, and that was something he'd not felt for a long time.

———

A s he made his way up the street to his home on Grapetree Lane, William was lost in another one of his daydreams. In this one, he was considering what kind of magical experiment he'd ask El Presto to perform if he was ever given the opportunity. He thought he might ask to be made the finest sportsman on earth. Or if that was too difficult, maybe he'd get motorised springs installed in his shoes so he could jump higher than everyone else... That would certainly be handy on the basketball court when he was playing for 'The Sharks'.

Better still, thought William, maybe El Presto could concoct some kind of super-serum, that would mix with his DNA and give him an amazing superpower. Like invisibility, laser-beam eyes, or x-ray vision...

But maybe he was being a little too unrealistic; after all, the chances of El Presto noticing him in the audience was practically zero. Plus, even just meeting El Presto in real-life would be like his birthday and Christmas rolled into one, and if he could get his DVD boxset signed by the famous science-magician that would be the real icing on the cake.

Rushing into his bedroom, the first thing William did (after a few minutes of bouncing up and down on his bed like a trampoline) was start collecting together all his memorabilia. Posters, DVDs, postcards, t-shirts, cuddly toys, board-games, collectible card-sets... If it had 'El Presto' printed on it, it was probably in William's collection somewhere.

He was buzzing, and as he dug through the cupboards and drawers in his room, he landed upon an old notepad that used to belong to his mum. He'd kept it because he felt it told him more about her character than anything else that had been left over after she died. And alongside the many shopping lists, doodles and short poems written inside, there was one memorable saying that she'd scribbled down in blue biro: "Life has many hurdles, you just need to learn how to jump over them."

William would sometimes recite this saying to himself, although never entirely sure of its meaning. He knew it was positive though, and because it was something that his mum believed in, that was enough for him. He was sure he'd come to understand it in time.

William stuffed all his El Presto memorabilia into the biggest sports bag he could find, slipped on his official glow-in-the-dark cap and leapt down the stairs excitedly.

Reaching the bottom, a tall, rake-thin shape stepped in his way.

"Where do you think you're going, William?" said *that* shrill voice. Then a long warty finger pointed right in his face.

It was Hilda.

"Oh, Hilda," William said, immediately feeling on edge as his stepmother loomed above him. "Um... I'm just going out to see a show with my friend."

"Since when did anyone want to be friends with *you*?" she replied bluntly.

"Um... Well, she's new to the school... And she's really nice, and I'm actually meeting her now, so I can't be late."

William gritted his teeth, finding it hard not to hide his frustration. He'd assumed the horrible woman was at the local bingo hall with the rest of her old cronies, like she usually was on a Friday night. Had she been, then William would've avoided the intense confrontation he was having right now. There she stood, in her dark, velvety, skin-hugging dress, like some nightmarish monstrosity from a Grimm's fairy tale.

Since the day she came into his life, William had refused to call Hilda 'Mother', 'Mummy', 'Mum', 'Ma' or any other variations of that maternal word. To him, she was simply the disgusting middle-aged lady that his father had chosen to marry (though William couldn't fathom why), and the person that happened to also live in his home (though he really wished she didn't).

Hilda had seemed nice at first and showered William with all kinds of gifts and sweet treats. Unfortunately, like

Dr. Jekyll turning himself into Mr. Hyde, she soon revealed her true self...

William hadn't seen it coming and was still annoyed at how blind he'd been to her act. He'd always thought that even though she would be no replacement for his mum, at least Hilda made his father happy. And William hadn't seen that for a long time.

However, the very next day after she'd walked down the aisle with his father, Hilda began moving all her many belongings into William's home. Boxes of antique junk, furniture, books, plants, and dozens and dozens of inky black candles. The house overflowed with her stuff; it was as though someone had removed any signs of his mum's existence, like a teacher wiping away scribbles on a white board.

In the chaos of Hilda's official arrival in his family home, William had struggled to rescue any of his mum's belongings. Fortunately, he had her notepad (which he stored away secretly), the comics (which William argued were rightfully his anyway), and her bed (which, as you know, was the most comfortable thing in the world to him). But from that day forward, things were never the same again. William would always feel like a stranger in the house he'd grown up in.

Hilda had a little mouth, screwed up like a full-stop, and greasy charcoal coloured hair, bundled up above her head in an untidy pile. She was also what you'd call 'consistent'. Consistently lazy, consistently grumpy, and consistently cruel... On their walk home, when Vanessa had asked William what she was like, he could only think of one word to describe her: *hideous*.

William's father was called Brian and he worked on an oil rig, far out in the middle of the ocean. He was at home so little that sometimes William felt he'd also died, at the same time as his mum. William often wondered whether his father had intentionally chosen to work so far away, so that he wouldn't have to be at home with his son. Or maybe, being in the same house where his wife once lived brought back too many sad memories for his father? William thought about this a lot, trying to find excuses for his father's absence, but all it did was make William feel even more lonely. And this feeling was worsened by Hilda, the evil witch that made no effort to be kind or motherly to him. He was trapped within her world and so often felt he could do absolutely nothing about it.

William's mum had passed away unexpectedly when he was 4-and-a-half years old, and though he was too young at the time to understand what was happening, the older he got the more he missed her and wished for her to still be part of his life. If he closed his eyes tightly and thought of nothing else, William could still feel the warmth of her hug, the softness of her skin, and the lavender smell of her perfume.

Sometimes he would see other children at school with their parents and would feel so jealous that his tummy would hurt. He had no photos, videos, or anything – aside from the notebook he'd secretly hidden in his drawer – to remind him of who his mum was. If he'd ever asked his dad about his mum, he would just get angry with William, and tell him to 'grow up.' William didn't understand that at all – he couldn't just *literally* change in height overnight. What did his father even mean?

H ilda scanned William with her horrible beady eyes, like some sort of alien robot from the *War of the Worlds* movie he'd once seen. William stared straight back as he slowly edged towards the front door, one small step at a time.

"What's in that bag you're carrying, boy?" she barked. Hilda had a horrible, scratchy voice, and one of those throaty wet coughs that could penetrate any wall in the house. You could always tell the room she was in if you just stopped to listen for a moment... "*HACCKKKKKKK*".

Bleugghhh. So gross.

"Oh, um, there's nothing much in the bag... Just some nerdy stuff that I wanted to show my new friend," said William.

"Well, that all sounds like a lot of nonsense to me... And you can't leave anyway," she sneered, "you've not yet sorted your dinner." Typically, Hilda seemed to be forgetting that it was *her* job as the grown-up to make his dinner. One thing William had discovered, right after she'd been legally made a part of his life, was that his existence was nothing more than an inconvenience to her.

William was right by the front door now. "I'm fine," he said, keeping his eyes trained on his stepmother. "I ate the rest of my lunchbox on the way home, so I'm not actually hungry."

He reached a hand towards the bronze-coloured door handle, knowing that if he didn't escape now, she'd find some absurd reason for him to have to stay. It was likely, based on previous experiences, that it'd be something like washing her pet poodle, Arthur, or cleaning the toilets with an old toothbrush, or watering the hundreds of flowers and plants she'd infested the house with.

Whatever it was, there was NO WAY he was missing the show tonight.

"The sooner you learn the better, my boy... If you live under *my* roof, you live by *my* rules. So, I think you should..."

SLAM!

William didn't even allow Hilda to finish her sentence before slamming the door behind him and scampering down the stone driveway. And by the time Hilda had managed to open the front door, William was already long gone.

4

THE BIG REVEAL

"Wow, your mum got us on the front row?" said William, as he and Vanessa took their seats in the auditorium.

"Yeah, and I didn't even want to ask her how much they cost," replied Vanessa, wrinkling her brow. "Although I'm guessing I'll be repaying her back in chores until I'm at least 30."

They had seats just by the end of the left side of the stage and were arguably both a little too short to be sat so close. William was already worrying about the potential neck-ache situation from having such a high viewing angle. But the benefit of being sat there also meant they'd be mere inches away from their hero once El Presto had taken the stage. And that was more than worth the pain.

Seeing the bag of merchandise William had with him, Vanessa nabbed William's glow-in-the-dark cap, cheekily telling him it was 'friend tax' for having to accompany him tonight. But he could tell that Vanessa was even more excited than he was. William watched as she scoured through the glossy programme she'd purchased in the foyer on the way in. "You know why I like El Presto?" said Vanessa, flipping through the pages. "It's because he's special. Absolutely nobody can do what he can do, and that makes him unique. Can you even imagine what that would be like? To know you're not like anybody else?"

William nodded in agreement but secretly wanted Vanessa to know that she was special herself, even if she couldn't make animals talk, shrink an elderly lady down to the size of a cat, or turn a kid into a blocky video-game character...

"Vanessa, you're spec..."

But no matter how sincere he wanted to be at that moment, he didn't get to finish his sentence. Vanessa touched her finger to his lips to shush him. "Don't say it... I know what you're going to say, and it's not true."

William knew not to go against her wishes, considering how stern she sounded. Plus, their friendship was so new he didn't want to seem like he was being too pushy or over-eager. Then again, he knew exactly how she felt. He *was* the definition of 'average', after all.

Vanessa's attention was now firmly on the stage. Her legs jiggled up and down in excitement. William turned to look back at the audience behind them and could see that every seat had now been filled.

The last time he'd been here was about 5 years ago, when his dad and Hilda had brought him to see a Christmas pantomime production of *Sleeping Beauty*. He grinned as he was reminded of how similar the Evil Queen was to his own evil stepmother Hilda... But his fondest memory was being selected to come up on-stage to be part of the show's finale. The princess (who had since gone on to be a major Hollywood star in her own superhero franchise, playing the character 'Fantastic Girl') gave him a basket of chocolates so vast he could barely carry it off-stage. Sweet treats had been such a rarity in his house since his mother had died that William made a point of eating the chocolates as slooooowly as humanly possible, and not sharing a single bite with Hilda (despite her attempted demands).

"We were lucky to get seats," said William. "Look at all the people here!"

"And this is my special treat for you," said Vanessa, smiling. "Think of it as a bonus for signing-on to be my new best friend."

William gave a bashful smirk. "Deal."

It was a rather grand theatre, with a large stage at one end and seating that curved around in a horse-shoe shape. The hundreds of seats were covered in a checked green and red fabric and were so old they'd become warped and bobbly. William found himself nervously picking off bits of material and had gathered a small pile in his right hand.

Vanessa looked at an empty chair beside her. "Have you noticed that you can see bottom-shaped imprints on the seats? Must be from all the people that have sat here over the years?"

"I really don't want to think about other people's bottoms," said William.

"Or all the farts that have been expelled on them?" smiled Vanessa wickedly.

"Ewww, you're so gross!" replied William, trying not to gag.

Suddenly the lights dimmed. Vanessa gripped a hand over her own mouth to stop herself from screaming out loud. They both sat unmoving, but Vanessa looked like a microwaved bag of popcorn, ready to explode.

At first, there was silence throughout the auditorium.

Then, the slow beat of drums...

boom, boom, boom.

Getting louder...

Boom, Boom, Boom....

And louder...

BOOM, BOOM, BOOM!

Now the audience began clapping in time.

The noise continued to build and got so loud that the whole building felt like it was shaking on its foundations.

Then suddenly...

CRASH!

The red curtains dropped from the front of the stage and standing there, under a bright spotlight, was the marvellous El Presto.

A medley of epic music played, blaring horns and thundering bass drums accompanying El Presto's big entrance. The audience erupted in a mighty roar, screaming his name and stamping their feet.

El Presto was dressed in a sequinned red tuxedo, with stars embroidered from the arms right down to the tail. Beneath his jacket he wore a pristine white shirt, but the most striking part of his outfit was his dazzling green bow tie. William thought El Presto looked a little bit smaller in real life, and perhaps a little older too. But the magician was extremely sprightly, sweeping across the stage, blowing kisses to his adoring fans as the glowing spotlight tracked along with him.

Finally, as the music began to die down and the audience hushed, he stepped towards the microphone. El Presto took a deep breath, straightened out his tie, then began to talk.

"Hello ladies, gentlemen and all you joyful children out there! I am of course the great El Presto, the science magician that makes the impossible possible!"

Another wild round of applause followed. Vanessa gave a high-pitched wolf-whistle so loud it drew the attention of El Presto himself. The magician stepped towards the edge of the stage, teetering above her, and crouched down close to her eye-level.

"Good evening young lady, and what would your name be?"

Vanessa gasped and instantly froze, like El Presto had clicked the Pause button on an invisible TV remote. She could feel her mouth drying up and had seemingly lost the ability to talk, too.

William nudged her in the ribs, hoping it might kick-start her back into life. Vanessa began to nod slowly, as she tried her very hardest to defrost herself and get some combination of words out: "Ummm... It's V-V-Van... Van-Van-Vane..."

"Vanessa!" William shouted on her behalf, trying to help.

"Ah, *Vanessa*. Such a lovely name! The name of my own grandmother,

no less... Now, would you like to help me kick off the show tonight?"

Vanessa's tongue felt like it was glued to the bottom of her mouth again, and she could only manage to bob her head up and down in affirmation.

Which she did.

A lot.

"Fantastic!" said El Presto as he turned from her and stepped back towards the middle of the stage. "Well Vanessa, all I need you to do is click your fingers. One little snap, and then the show can begin!" He whirled back to her one last time. "Think you can do it?"

Vanessa glanced to William, clearly still needing some help to process what was happening. He gave her a wink of approval and whispered: "Go on. Do it."

Vanessa raised her right hand, clasped her thumb and middle finger together, and...

CLICK!

Suddenly the whole stage lit up behind El Presto, sending the audience into rapturous applause.

Vanessa, whose smile couldn't possibly go any wider if she tried, was entranced by the wondrous stage design which, prior to the click of her fingers, had been shrouded in total darkness.

The newly lit stage revealed a formation of red bulbs, hung high above, which William realised spelt out the name of EL PRESTO. He then noticed the dozens of tall transparent canisters that stood in a semicircle around the back and sides of the stage. Each one contained a slimy green liquid that oozed and bubbled. Plastic pipes of different shapes and sizes connected the containers together, as the bogey-green substance bubbled and flowed between each one.

Various animals in cages also littered the stage: parrots; dogs; mice; a pig; a horse; a llama; a goat; a wolf, and a crocodile that must've been over 6 feet long. The crocodile snapped its jaw shut as El Presto threw it a sloppy chunk of red meat.

As the audience settled, El Presto began to speak again. "Tonight, I'll be showing you something that you'll have never seen before." He walked backwards and forwards across the stage, talking with great confidence. Sometimes, he would leave big pauses between his sentences for dramatic effect.

"You will see the result of my latest scientific experiment... A feat so extraordinary that even *I* can't believe it's possible."

By now, Vanessa and William were so close to the edge of their seats they were practically falling off.

El Presto continued. "When I was a child... I was a rather strange little boy with barely any friends. I would play on my own for much of the time, performing magic shows to my teddy bears... But after a while, I started to realise I might be different from other children. It worried me at first, I must admit... But my clever mother told me that *I should never be afraid of the things that make me different*. She said I needed to be brave, embrace it, and make that part of who I am. Those things will ultimately be what defines me in life."

El Presto stopped for a moment and took a sip from a glass of water on a stool beside him. The audience watched and listened, totally captivated, as he owned the stage.

"The point I'm getting to, as many fans of mine across the world know, is I like to be a little *adventurous* with my magic. I try to break boundaries... I try to shock and awe... I try to be... ExperiMENTAL!"

The people were on their feet; the enigmatic magician having now managed to work his audience into a complete frenzy. El Presto waved at them, asking for calm and for them to retake their seats. He had so much power over them in this very moment, that they did it almost instantaneously.

"But everyone... I know you're not here to listen to me regale stories of my childhood, or for me to be telling you how simply magnificent I am... You've all bought tickets for this show tonight because you want to see what *new* trickery I have up my sleeve!"

Vanessa nodded her head feverishly and whispered the quietest of whispers to William: "What do you think he's going to do?"

William shrugged, unsure. But he guessed it probably involved animals, considering how many lined the stage. It would probably also involve that mysterious icky green goo.

As he talked, El Presto strode over to the llama, which was strapped to one of the canisters by a leash. He stroked its back and tickled its chin. Vanessa could swear she saw the animal smile.

"However," El Presto said, "before I can show you my

latest unbelievable creation, I need to ask you all... How many have seen my *talking fish experiment*?"

Of course, *everyone* had. And everyone raised their hand. With 14,025,527,981 views, it was the most watched video on YouTube.

"Brilliant! Well, since that performance I've worked tirelessly in my laboratory to push what's possible with the mind of an animal. Science has shown that many creatures can communicate with one another, in ways that we are yet to truly understand. And that is what inspired my original experiment. But I thought, what would happen if we could go one step further? What if an animal could not only talk with us, but also *walk* amongst us?"

Again, another overly dramatic pause.

By now, there were audible whispers among the audience, who were struggling to contain their anticipation.

"So... time for the unveiling..." El Presto signalled to a man at the back of the room controlling the stage sound effects. "Drumroll please!"

Rat-a-tat-a-tat-a-tat-a-tat-a-tat-a-tat-a-tat-a-tat-a-tat-a-tat-a...

William and Vanessa slapped their knees in time with the drumroll, which was getting faster, and faster, and faster...

"Presenting... my cybernetic masterpiece... *FISHNIP!*"

The drumroll stopped with a huge crashing cymbal.

Then stage lights flashed brightly in red, yellow and blue.

The centre of the floor began to creak as it slowly slid open.

Fog billowed out dramatically, filling almost the entire stage.

And from the opening appeared something metallic.

It seemed to rise from the stage-floor, like it was levitating.

Then what followed was a strange mechanical *whirring* noise...

Then *bleeping, blooping* and *clanging*...

Suddenly the stage lights blinked off, and a single spotlight shone down on something tall in the middle of the stage.

Something shiny, something robotic... with a *fishbowl* for a head?

The audience murmured as they tried to understand what they were seeing before them. William and Vanessa could hear what a lot of them were saying:

"A robot?"

"Wait, is that a glass bowl where its head should be?"

"And there's a goldfish swimming around in it?"

"No, it can't be... It's not scientifically possible!"

"How has El Presto done it?"

It took William a second to comprehend what he was seeing, then it hit him. He leapt to his feet and screamed. "OMG!"

Vanessa quickly followed and stood up beside him, putting her arm around his shoulders. "It's a freaking robot!" she exclaimed.

"With a fishbowl for a head?" replied William.

Vanessa simply couldn't believe it. "Can that fish control the robot?"

"No, surely not... That wouldn't be possible..."

But it *could* control the robot.

And it did.

The machine, which stood several feet taller than El Presto, walked across the stage. Its metal feet clinked and clanged as it stomped. Lights flickered and flashed in patterns on its bulbous chest. Amazingly, whatever direction the fish faced the robot went there too. It was like the fish was steering the robot with its mind, or with an invisible joystick.

Now another spotlight turned on, and El Presto stood in a pose as if to say 'ta-dah'!

An applause rippled through the auditorium.

"Thank you, thank you!" he said, taking a bow.

After soaking up the claps and cheers for a bit longer, El Presto beckoned for everyone to sit down again.

"This is **FISHNIP 2.0** – a walking, talking fish-bot." El Presto pointed towards his latest creation as it continued to walk around the stage.

The fish-bot seemed extremely pleased with itself and, like El Presto, was enjoying this moment in the spotlight. Audience members took photos, recorded it with their camera-phones and snapped selfies as the robot posed for them. They were collectively stunned when Fishnip cartwheeled and flipped into the air like an Olympic gymnast. Dust rose from the stage as he landed with a cool super-hero-type pose, drilling his fist into the floor.

SLAM!

The audience roared, climbing to their feet once more. William and Vanessa stood on their chairs, screaming so loudly it made their throats hurt. They were in wonderment of El Presto's latest science-magic and knew they were witnessing history in the making. Once again, he'd made the impossible possible!

El Presto walked to the front of the stage and held out the microphone before him.

CLANG!

He dropped the mic, causing a ripple of feedback to screech and echo throughout the theatre.

El Presto gazed out at the awestruck crowd, with the knowledge that by the time this performance had wrapped up, he would not only be talk of the town, but of the planet too. However, for all those nights where El Presto had lain in bed trying to imagine this very moment and the positive effect it would have across the world of science, and all the GIFS and memes that would be shared online featuring his ground-breaking work, he hadn't considered what would happen if things didn't *quite* go to plan...

But unfortunately, he was about to find out.

5

FISH OUT OF THEATRE

El Presto could see the inevitable headlines already:
'World's greatest magician stuns crowd with latest creation!'

'El Presto is el besto, in new science stunner!'

'Best mic drop ever, as El Presto reveals his career defining masterpiece!'

This was *his* moment. El Presto could feel in his bones that when he left the stage tonight, everything would change. Everything he'd ever done in his career was leading up to this unveiling, and it was going even better than expected. He would be viral within the hour, with #ElPresto trending on every social media platform there was. TV chat shows would be begging to interview him. Then there were all the radio stations and podcasts he'd be asked to appear on. EVERYONE would be talking about him.

And he was exactly right.

But unfortunately, people would be talking about him for completely different reasons... Because as El Presto departed the stage to a standing ovation, something *very bad and unexpected happened...*

To everyone's horror, Fishnip stole the microphone and began to address the audience... And what he said next, would send a shockwave of chills throughout the auditorium:

"I AM DR. FISHNIP. AND I AM HERE TO GET PAYBACK!!! ALL YOU HUMANS OUT THERE, THAT HAVE DELIGHTED IN EATING MY FELLOW BROTHERS AND SISTERS, ARE NOW ABOUT TO LEARN WHAT IT FEELS LIKE TO BE SOMEONE ELSE'S DINNER!"

Since the last experiment, Fishnip's language had improved immensely, and with El Presto's patented 'TRANSLOPEDIA 500' now integrated into the fishbowl, he had no problem communicating to the audience exactly what he was thinking.

William turned to Vanessa. "Um... Is that robot fish threatening to eat all of us?"

Vanessa looked back at William, clearly alarmed at the drama unfolding in front of them. "I think so? I mean, honestly I think I'm going to need you to pinch me, because I'm dreaming, right? This isn't actually happening *right now*, is it?"

"And what did he call himself? Dr. Fishnip?" asked William.

"Yeah... But a doctor of what?"

"I mean, all goldfish do is swim around in circles, eat fish flakes and shoot out long stringy poops. So, your guess is as good as mine."

Seeing all the sudden hullabaloo, El Presto rushed back onto the stage, as surprised as anyone with this turn of events. But as he did so, Dr. Fishnip was prepared...

A squirt of black oil shot from a small compartment on the robot's bottom, landing with a SPLOSH on the wooden floorboards. Before El Presto could react, he found himself slipping and sliding right off the stage and landing on a group of people on the front row.

"Ooops, sorry!" he said, embarrassed. He puffed and panted as he climbed off the pile of fans below him.

"HAHA! DO NOT ATTEMPT TO STOP ME, EL PRESTO! FROM THIS DAY FORWARD, FISH SHALL RULE THE EARTH!" shouted Dr. Fishnip, before spinning away. The robot clanged and whirred as chains and gears operated inside him. He dashed to the back of the stage, feet crashing down on the stage floor. In a split-second, he'd disappeared, whilst also managing to snatch two of the green canisters on his way out – one under each arm.

Before William could react, Vanessa did something very spontaneous and perhaps a little... No, it wasn't *a little crazy*, it wasn't even *half crazy*, it was absolutely positively *100% crazy*.

Vanessa had decided that she would bravely pursue Dr. Fishnip, and William could only watch in amazement as his new friend hopped up onto the stage like a kangaroo, dodged the oil slick with a balletic leap, and sprinted after him like a greyhound chasing a rabbit.

"What am I going to do?" considered William, feeling quite breathless all of a sudden. He couldn't just leave Vanessa to tackle Fishnip alone. Nor did he think he could be of any real assistance because:

1. He was only 13, and this seemed like a job for grown-ups or the police.

2. Dr. Fishnip had the body of a technologically advanced robot, which meant any attempt to stop him would probably result in William ending up in a lot of pain.

3. He'd seen that Fishnip had a few tricks up his sleeves (e.g. oil slick spray) and knew there was probably more where that came from.

4. He was *very, very scared*.

But William also had a brave streak, something he'd realised last year when he decided to walk through a haunted funhouse attraction alone on Halloween to prove to his awful stepmother Hilda that he wasn't a 'massive scaredy cat'.

Actually, he *was* extremely scared on that occasion too, but he'd do absolutely anything to prove that spiteful stinking witch wrong. So, at this very moment, with his new best friend Vanessa hot on the heels of that huge menacing fish-bot, he knew he had no choice but to find that level of bravery again and help her.

William sprang up and screamed Vanessa's name in the vain hope she might hear him and reconsider her perilous pursuit ... But Vanessa was also extremely determined; William had already learned that about her just from the truly short amount of time they'd spent together today.

The reality was Vanessa had no intention of giving up whatsoever, even if it meant she was in great danger...

Which of course, she certainly *was*...

6

THE SECRET OF THE OOZE

A short while later, William and Vanessa found El Presto backstage in his dressing room, being treated for a painful looking graze on his head. A nurse was applying a large plaster as he winced at the pain from his fall.

"Just keep still sir, I've almost finished," said the nurse impatiently as El Presto wriggled in his chair.

William and Vanessa slowly approached the magician, who hadn't seen either of them enter the room.

Vanessa leant in and warily touched El Presto on the shoulder. The nerves she felt at being so close to her hero made her belly feel like a tumble dryer full of butterflies. "Erm... Mr. El Presto? W-W-We're the ones that chased down Dr. Fishnip."

El Presto spun around to look at his guests. But to their surprise he didn't seem too pleased to see them... He scanned them up and down slowly, clearing his throat as he did so. The first thing that was most obvious to him, was that Vanessa and William were drenched in his patented green ooze – so much so it was dripping onto the floor and forming a slimy pool around them.

As El Presto began to comprehend what he was seeing, the magician's face turned ghostly white. "Oh dear. Oh deary dear... That's not what I think it is... Is it?" he asked.

"If you're thinking that this is *your* green ooze that we're covered in, then yes that's exactly what it is," replied William, soggy and unimpressed.

El Presto leapt to his feet, taking the nurse by surprise. He began to walk back and forth in a panic, muttering to himself, scratching his head, then his chin, and at one point both at the same time.

"Are you okay Mr. Presto?" asked William, concerned at the magician's sudden and strong reaction.

"Y-Y-Yes. No... Um, I don't know..." he replied. Beads of sweat were now dripping off his face.

"Should we be concerned?" Vanessa asked. "I mean, that's certainly the vibe I'm getting right now."

El Presto shook his head, then quickly changed his mind and nodded. "Well, let's put it like this. That green ooze is... *unpredictable*. It can do things... Very *strange* things, that even I can't imagine."

"I don't understand. You made it, right? Surely *you* control what it can do?" asked William, letting the sentence hang there for a second.

El Presto looked to the nurse, then pointed at the door. "You can't hear this. It's confidential. Please, you have to leave us."

Annoyed at El Presto's blunt manner, the nurse picked up her medical bag, went to the door and left the room. But not before giving it an almighty *SLAM*, just to let everyone know how displeased she was at being asked to leave at the most interesting point in the story.

"I have to say, that was a bit rude of you Mr. El Presto," said Vanessa.

Surprisingly, El Presto nodded in agreement. "Yes I know, it's just that time is of the essence right now and we can't have anyone else hearing what I'm about to tell you. It's not only highly confidential, but it's the biggest secret in *all magic*. You have to promise not to share it with anyone!"

"We won't tell," said Vanessa, as she stood uncomfortably in her damp, goopy clothes. Globs of the green stuff continued to drip to the floor.

"We promise," agreed William.

"Good, I just can't have any of this getting out. My whole career would be in ruins," puffed El Presto, looking sick with worry. Vanessa wondered whether it might've been safer for the nurse to stick around after all, just in case.

"So," asked William, "are you going to tell us what's happening? That green ooze of yours that powers so much of your magic... The stuff we're both *completely* covered in... What exactly is it?"

El Presto began to stride around the room again, considering the scale of the story he was about to share, and how the children might react. "You might not believe this, but I found the ooze in a small glass capsule. In a *spaceship*."

William and Vanessa were so shocked by this revelation, that if this had been a Looney Tunes cartoon their jaws would've dropped to the ground like anvils.

"Wait... What?" exclaimed Vanessa.

"It sounds unbelievable, I know. But when I was a child, living on a farm in the middle of the countryside, an alien spacecraft crashed in a field behind my house. Nobody knew about it, only my parents and me. Unfortunately, the strange blobby-like alien creature that we found inside had died. I can only assume his ship had been floating around in space and, after entering our atmosphere, eventually crash-landed on Earth."

William shook his head and took a seat beside El Presto. "You're trying to trick us, aren't you? I mean, that's what you do. That's your whole *shtick.*"

El Presto shook his head., "Unfortunately not this time, kids. Look, I know how this sounds. At first, I thought my parents were playing a prank on me too. But nope, there it was... A real alien spacecraft, more or less crash-landed in my back-garden. My father didn't know what to do, so he buried the ship deep in the soil. He was worried a secret division of government agents might descend upon us, and wipe our memories or, even worse, lock us away and experiment on us... But before my father put it underground I managed to sneak inside and steal a capsule of the alien's fuel."

"And I'm assuming their fuel is what we're both covered in right now?" replied William.

El Presto nodded sheepishly. "Sort of, yes".

"But there were dozens of canisters of that stuff on stage, wasn't there?' asked Vanessa.

"Yes, you're correct," replied El Presto. "I spent years reverse engineering the ooze, eventually learning how to create the formula and harnessing its magical properties for myself. I then dedicated my life to manufacturing more of it... As much as I possibly could."

"So how much did you make exactly?" William said.

"Gallons and gallons of it, which I store in a secret, secure location. There might be a hundred vats full of it. I've lost count. The main thing is, it stays hidden away so it can't fall into the wrong hands."

Vanessa shook her head "Um... You mean like Dr. Fishnip?"

El Presto nodded sadly, "Yes, correct... just like Fishnip." El Presto then had a sudden moment of realisation. "But... you said you managed to stop him, correct?"

Vanessa looked to the floor sadly. "Well, not exactly... That's the reason we're here now."

7

VANISHED!

El Presto, William and Vanessa entered the alleyway at the back of the theatre and gathered around a broken canister of slime. On the brick wall above, a lightbulb shone down, casting their huge shadows across the cobblestone street. William knelt over, inspecting the puddle of green oozy stuff before them.

"Dr. Fishnip was attempting to steal it from you, El Presto," said William. "He grabbed two canisters as he made his escape, but thanks to Vanessa's quick thinking we managed to stop him... *Temporarily*, at least."

As they walked further along the narrow walkway, William and Vanessa went on to explain, in extensive detail, what happened in in the moments following Dr. Fishnip's escape. So much detail, that El Presto was secretly wishing he could hit a fast forward button and get to the good bits.

Vanessa explained how, in her pursuit through the dark areas behind the stage, she'd snatched a roll of rope and quickly fashioned a small lasso with it. With precise aim she'd managed to skilfully sling the lasso under one of Dr. Fishnip's bionic legs. But rather than stopping him, she found herself being helplessly dragged out the exit doors and into the stony alleyway that led to Fishnip's potential freedom.

Determined not to let go, she could only watch as Dr. Fishnip made his attempt to wriggle free of the rope. In kicking out his leg – and likely also down to him still not having fully mastered the control of his robotic limbs – Fishnip had accidentally dropped one of the glass canisters, which cracked as it impacted on the hard floor.

Vanessa described the moment of panic, where Fishnip could only watch as the green slime splashed across the cobblestones, creating a large pool of thick, sticky goo between them both. But as the robo-fish realised he still had one canister left, he took the opportunity to deliver an unbelievably precise and powerful karate chop, finally slicing himself free of the rope.

"HA! NOTHING CAN STOP ME!" mimicked Vanessa, clearly impressing William with her Dr. Fishnip imitation skills.

But El Presto was becoming impatient at this unnecessarily drawn-out retelling of events. "And then he escaped?" the magician asked.

"Not quite," replied Vanessa. "But what happened next was *brilliant*."

El Presto rolled his eyes, as he found himself itching at the irritating plaster on his forehead.

"Fishnip hadn't seen the brick wall behind him," Vanessa laughed, "and as he spun around he smashed straight into it and clattered to the floor in a big metal heap. Honestly, I'm surprised the whole fishbowl didn't topple off and smash."

"But that still doesn't explain how you ended up like

this" said El Presto, pointing his finger at the children's slime-drenched clothes.

"Well, due to the momentum of Fishnip's karate chop, and the fact I was already being pulled along like a water skier, I couldn't stop myself from sliding straight into the puddle of slime. It completely covered me, and I couldn't shake it off at all."

"Like when you get a bogey you can't flick off your finger," added William.

"Exactly," Vanessa agreed. "And when William finally arrived, and saw me splatted within the goo, he tried to help me up."

"But I've never had good balance. Mum always said that's why she stopped my gymnastics classes. As I was helping Vanessa up I could feel my own feet slipping..."

"So *you* fell into it too," confirmed El Presto, trying his hardest not to roll his eyes in frustration.

"Affirmative," said William.

But as they continued to walk towards the end of the alleyway, El Presto found himself becoming increasingly confused. "Fishnip's escape... Your attempts to stop him... All of that I understand... But that still doesn't explain why Fishnip isn't here now?"

As they inspected the scene, the frustration on El Presto's face was clear. He looked at the children, exasperated. But the frustration he felt wasn't because *they'd* failed, but because *he* had failed in seeing this all happening in the first place.

William pointed towards the makeshift weapons they'd used. "We bashed him repeatedly with those metal bin lids to ensure he wouldn't get away."

"But when we turned around—"

"—he had vanished."

Vanessa screwed up her face and crossed her arms. "What a total mess. We're so sorry, El Presto."

El Presto had a glum look on his face. "I can't believe he's *finally* managed to get away."

"Finally?" replied Vanessa.

"Yes," replied El Presto. "He's tried this before when he was just my pet fish in a bowl. Honestly, I lost count of the escape attempts. He was becoming too clever for me, but I'd hoped that I'd finally gotten through to him after the last time."

"What happened the last time?" questioned William, narrowing his eyes.

"He'd built up so much momentum in his tank that he managed to knock it over completely. It smashed to the ground, and within the pools of water he was able to wriggle his way through a grate in the floor of my workshop. What he hadn't accounted for was the system of ventilation fans running under the floor. Had I not managed to catch him in my net just in time, he'd have been sliced into sushi."

"And this is the thanks you get? What an absolute monster," said Vanessa.

"Yes, but then he is *my* creation after all... I'm responsible for him, which means I need to make sure I get him back without injury."

"Without injury to Fishnip, or... *someone else*?" asked William.

El Presto raised his eyebrows and pursed his lips, not quite ready to admit the danger the city was now in.

William couldn't help but think how different El Presto seemed away from the stage. No longer the confident, bubbly celebrity that was known for wowing the world with his science-defying magic. Here, he seemed just like anyone else and for William that felt strangely comforting. He *was* just a normal person after all.

"We can help!" Vanessa shouted excitedly.

"Listen kids, I greatly appreciate the offer, and what you've already done for me. So as a thank you I'll happily sign all of your memorabilia with a 15% discounted fee."

"Um, thanks?" said William, knowing the offer wasn't particularly generous, all things considered.

"I just need to do this alone now. I can't have anyone else getting hurt, especially not children. And Fishnip has already proven to be completely unpredictable. He's still got one of my canisters, and it's up to me alone to stop the little monster."

"Fine," replied Vanessa with a shrug of resignation.

"But just make sure you go straight home and get that stuff washed off your skin," said El Presto. "If it can turn a fish into an evil mastermind, imagine what it could do to you guys!" He sounded like he was joking at first, but as his voice tailed off William realised El Presto was probably hiding how scared he really was.

"Anyway, I'd best go find a mop to clear this mess up." And with that El Presto disappeared back down the alley-way, and through the doors into the theatre. He looked deep in thought, and deeply troubled.

Vanessa and William looked back to the canister and the puddle of green ooze. It bubbled and steamed on the cold floor. Then they looked to their own discoloured skin, and the way the ooze was starting to crust up like dried mud.

"I think I should go home and have a hot bath," said William.

"Yeah, I think we'll need plenty of soap and washing powder to get this yucky stuff off," replied Vanessa as she looked down to her soaking wet clothes.

8

A MONSTROUS AWAKENING

The following morning William wiped his tired eyes and slid out of bed. He didn't know what time it was, but really it didn't matter because today was Saturday and he had nothing very important to do. Nor did he have to fear being dragged out of bed by Hilda, as she normally slept in until lunchtimes on the weekend.

As William sat perched on his bed, he considered that he was pretty okay with having a clear diary today, especially when he looked at his pile of unplayed video games. Having recently traded in one of his father's vintage consoles for a much higher price than he'd expected, he'd been able to update his games library with a host of new titles...

Question was, which one would he play first? In the pile were some remakes of older games, as well as some recent classics such as:

- *Super Marian Sisters*
- *Pingy the Porcupine*
- *Call of Doody*

- *Call of Doody: Brown Ops*
- *Super Marian Kart*
- *Hay-man*
- *Granny Theft Auto*
- *Un-farted*
- *Bed Head Redemption*
- *Mortal Wombat*
- *Plants vs. Donkeys*

So many choices!

William yawned, mouth stretching unusually wide, and got to his feet.

He banged his head on the ceiling light.

CLANG!

Wait... *the ceiling light?*

William peered down to the floor. It seemed to be much further away from him than normal, which he realised probably meant that he was now a bit taller than yesterday. Had he grown in the night? It was likely; he'd read in a biology book that you tend to do most of your growing when you go to sleep... But surely not THIS much? William was always one of the shorter kids in his school year, so the sudden and dramatic change in height was unsettling.

But not quite as unsettling as when he saw his toes...

Then his legs...

His hands...

And his arms.

They were GREEN...

And SCALY too!

William crept over to the mirror slowly, not quite understanding what was happening, and a little scared for what he might see in the reflection.

The first thing that came into view was his long snout. Then, as William gasped he revealed dozens of sharp teeth in his mouth. They looked as though they could chew through even the toughest of meats. As he rubbed his skin, it no longer felt soft and fleshy. Instead, it was tough, thick and rugged.

"No, it can't be..." William uttered quietly, careful not to wake his stepmother in the next room. It felt a little weird to talk, his mouth no longer having lips, and his jaw now long and flapping. As he stood there, he could barely believe the words that were about to come out of his mouth: **"I've turned into a crocodile!"**

9

A GIRL IN WOLF'S CLOTHING

On the other side of the city, Vanessa was also waking up. She pulled back the duvet and checked her alarm clock, and saw it was 11.30 a.m. and 48 seconds. Last night's activities had really taken it out of her, she thought to herself, as she blinked the tiredness from her eyes.

Vanessa stretched her arms and yawned the biggest yawn ever. But the sound that left her mouth was not quite what she expected...

Hooooooooowwwwl!

Vanessa shot up, startled. That didn't *sound* right...

That sounded like an *animal*...

But how did SHE make that noise?

Maybe her voice was just a bit croaky as she hadn't used it yet today?

Unless...

Vanessa looked down at her hands. At least, where her hands *should've* been... Instead, there were soft brown paws, pointy black claws, and thick, bristly grey fur.

"What on Earth?" she snarled.

Vanessa blinked a few more times and rubbed her eyes. Maybe her mind was playing tricks...

That's right, she was hallucinating. Or perhaps she was dreaming? That had to be it!

But no...

This wasn't like the time where she dreamt she was the leader of a ragtag group of survivors, fighting off a horde of zombies as she defended the last fried chicken shop on Earth. (She'd awoken from that dream punching her wall so hard the dents were still there as a reminder.)

This was really *happening*.

Vanessa touched a paw towards her mouth, or at least where her mouth *should've been*. Instead, there was a cold round black nose, a long fluffy snout, and a collection of sharp, pointy teeth.

Vanessa gasped and — quick as a flash — rushed out of her bedroom, across the landing and straight into the bathroom. She slammed the door behind her and fastened the lock; a job made much more difficult now she had paws instead of hands.

There was no way her family could see her like this. Vanessa could picture her father now, pointing a sharp kitchen knife at her and telling her to 'get out', like some kind of dangerous rabid animal. The thought was terrifying.

Vanessa closed her eyes, positioned herself in front of the mirror, and took a big, deep breath. As she exhaled, she opened her eyes and saw...

Her worst nightmare...

SHE WAS A WOLF!

Vanessa resisted the urge to scream, afraid the noise might come out as a howl again.

Her mind raced, accelerating through all the possibilities: *This can't be happening. I'm dreaming. It's impossible. Nobody really turns into an animal?! This is real-life after all, not a fantasy like Harry Potter... Am I a werewolf? Like Remus Lupin? No, I don't think so, after all, werewolves tend to attack humans, and I wouldn't hurt a fly... Maybe it's temporary like when a vampire turns into a bat? Maybe it'll fade away and tomorrow I'll wake up and be normal again? Werewolves don't stay werewolves, right?*

Vanessa glanced down at her fur-covered body. A mix of thick brown and grey hair covered every single part of her. Vanessa momentarily considered powering up her dad's electric shaver, but then had visions of it going wrong and her ending up looking like a badly groomed poodle.

Then she glanced over to the toilet. How would she use *that* now? Could she go even to the toilet? Would she have to cock her leg up like a dog? *No, only boy dogs did that...* Well, she didn't need to go right now anyway, so maybe that was one less thing to be concerned about for the time being.

RIIIINNNNNNG!

Vanessa spun around, hearing her mobile phone in the bedroom.

She slowly undid the lock on the bathroom door and crept out into the landing, one small step at a time. Every creak in the floorboards felt like an earthquake to her; she feared disturbing her parents and couldn't even begin to fathom what would happen if they caught sight of her in this monstrous form...

But thankfully no-one heard her, and as she entered her bedroom, she closed the door softly behind her.

Her phone was still ringing, and upon picking it up she saw the name WILLIAM displayed in large white text on the screen. Vanessa hesitated at first, not wanting her sudden transformation to ruin her burgeoning new friendship. But then she supposed, *after the events of last night, if I can tell anyone about this, it's William.*

Vanessa reached out a paw and touched the green answer button.

"Hello," she said quietly, placing the phone against one of her long ears.

A deep voice replied, surprising Vanessa. "Hello? Um... It's William... Um, I've got something I need to tell you. It's extremely strange and... *unbelievable*... and you're going to think I'm joking, or that I'm as mad as a box of frogs, but..."

"Stop right there," said Vanessa. "Have you woken up this morning, perhaps looking a little ummm... *different* than last night?"

"Um... Yeah. You could certainly say that."

"And would you say that your appearance is now a little more... *animalistic* perhaps?"

"Wait," replied William, "don't say you also..."

"Yep," interrupted Vanessa, her eyes brightening as she immediately realised she wasn't going to have to face this strange and scary situation on her own.

"Let's meet up. RIGHT. NOW."

10

TRANSFORMATION EXCLAMATION

William and Vanessa arranged to meet in the nearby woods, but knew they'd have to wait until it got dark. They deduced that it was highly unlikely anyone would be there at night, perhaps just the odd dog walker or two, so it was a much safer bet than meeting in either one of their houses, or somewhere in the middle of Cruz City.

William and Vanessa were knelt beside each other, tactically positioned behind the stump of a rotten old oak tree. In truth, they weren't that well-hidden, as they were still yet to come to terms with just how physically bigger they were in their new animal forms.

From the moment they'd arrived at their meeting place in Heartland Forest, they'd struggled to find the right words to explain their mind-boggling predicament. There was a lot to discuss, not least the fact that William had chosen to wear his mother's long pink dressing gown to disguise his appearance, or that Vanessa had wrapped herself in a variety of multi-coloured blankets, like a rubbish Obi-Wan Kenobi. The first thing to talk about, however, was how on earth could this have all happened?

"Remember last night, when we were at the El Presto show?" said Vanessa.

"Yep."

"And remember what happened when we chased Fishnip?"

"We got covered in the ooze?"

"It drenched us, probably seeped into our skin, did something weird to our DNA. El Presto did warn us... And I even had a two-hour bath to try and wash it all off but looks like we weren't fast enough."

"Oh my, that *must* be what happened," realised William. "That stuff in the canister... It's transformed us!"

"We need to find El Presto immediately, he'll know what to do," said Vanessa assuredly.

"But how are we going to find him with us looking like *this*?" worried William. "It's not like we can just stroll along the street and expect people not to see us. What would you think if you saw a giant crocodile and wolf passing you by as you did your weekly shop?"

Vanessa considered this for a moment, then had a thought: "El Presto told us that you should never be afraid of the thing that makes you *different*. He said you should be brave, embrace it."

But William wasn't so convinced. "Yeah, although I don't think he was referring to this *specific* situation."

"No," replied Vanessa, "but I think he's correct and we shouldn't be scared right now. This is totally bonkers, and people *will* be shocked when they see us, but this is who we are now, and we simply need to deal with it."

William nodded in agreement. "You're right," he said. In fact he was beginning to learn that Vanessa was *nearly* always right. And though she could be a little rash in her decision making, like chasing Fishnip last night, she clearly had a great knack for adapting to any situation.

"By the way William, your voice is super deep, now. You sound like a grown-up... Probably a good thing, though, right? I mean, imagine looking like that..." Vanessa pointed a finger directly at him, "and sounding like a squeaky little kid."

William laughed, letting out a *snort* from the big nostrils at the end of his snout. "Oh sorry, I didn't know I could make that sound." He squirmed a little, feeling embarrassed.

Vanessa tried to hide her smile at first, but it was useless.

She broke out in a fit of giggles, losing her balance and falling into the pile of crisp green leaves to the side of her.

Now they both laughed.

"By the way William," said Vanessa with a cheeky smile, "the bald look really suits you."

"At least I've not got a hairy bottom," joked William in return.

Vanessa wagged her tail feverishly. It flapped from side to side, slapping the mossy soil she sat on. "Well, that's certainly new," she said, wide-eyed.

Suddenly, they heard a SHRIEK!

But it didn't sound human...

It sounded like an animal of some kind...

An animal in a lot of *pain*.

In a split-second, Vanessa leapt to her feet. Then, before William could say a word, she was gone. She'd bolted, as fast as a Formula 1 racing car, and was now just a blur in the distance.

"Blimey, not again!" exclaimed William, feeling a sense of déjà vu. He got to his feet, and begun to give chase, "wait for me!"

11

MEANWHILE AT AQUAWORLD...

Dr. Fishnip had been deeply excited for El Presto's show, knowing what was to follow. He'd been on his best behaviour through all the build-up and rehearsals, which was one of the reasons El Presto was so taken by surprise during the actual live show. The last El Presto expected was for his latest and greatest trick to turn on him in such a dastardly way.

El Presto's stage production had been a long time in the making, but then so had Dr. Fishnip's own carefully engineered and highly secretive plans.

Weeks before the big night, Fishnip had hijacked a number of El Presto's online shopping accounts, ordered a whole host of different items and had everything delivered to a secret location. By accessing El Presto's Wi-Fi through the robot's internal router, Dr. Fishnip had been given access to the entire Internet, and he'd used that as an opportunity to secretly plot against his creator.

At night, when El Presto slept, Fishnip would be drawing and testing and engineering, learning how to be the best super-villain imaginable. Fishnip had learnt so much during his research that he could've written his own best-selling book – *101 Tips on Becoming the World's Greatest Bad Guy* – if he'd really wanted. But Fishnip wasn't looking to become an author, at least not quite yet (perhaps when he needed some money to invest in more laser guns).

Dr. Fishnip had planned the execution of his escape very carefully and had already decided on his eventual destination, once he was free of his owner. That night in the theatre, everything was coordinated and executed to perfection, with such detail and precision that even El Presto couldn't help but be secretly impressed with what the little goldfish had managed to achieve.

Through all his planning, the biggest issue for Fishnip was finding a place he could infiltrate in order to set up the next stage of his world takeover. He'd need somewhere that had lots of space, easy access to other aquatic life, and an abundance of delicious food (e.g. fish flakes, his favourite snack). It didn't take long for Fishnip to realise the perfect venue in Cruz City for his bad-guy lair:

AQUAWORLD DISCOVERY AND FUN CENTRE.

Flashback to two years ago, El Presto had paid a visit to Aquaworld as part of the TV series *Secrets of the Astonishing El Presto: Revealed*, and during a live episode was gifted a fish by the park's owners. It was given as a thank you for his charity work and support of aquatic welfare. The gift of course was a goldfish, and El Presto accepted it with much gratitude.

Over time El Presto became quite attached to this fish, which had a cheeky habit of trying to nip at his fingers when it was feeding time. El Presto had always imagined the conversations he might have with little *Fishnip*, seeing as his pet appeared to have such a strong personality (rarely seen in fish), and so as his science and magic evolved, he committed to trying to find a way to give Fishnip a voice of his own. This would be his first mistake...

Because Aquaworld was once his home, it seemed like a no-brainer for Dr. Fishnip to return there to enact the next stage of his plans. And for many weeks prior to his arrival, staff at Aquaworld had been receiving deliveries of large boxes that they'd been instructed to store in a certain area of the park. Nobody had bothered to question what the boxes were for, or what they contained, perhaps assuming that plans were afoot for a major new park upgrade. The staff were rarely ever told of future expansions to Aquaworld, and so they simply thought nothing of it and carried on their usual duties.

Like the famous theme park in Orlando with the big-eared mouse for a mascot, Aquaworld had a network of secret underground tunnels and rooms that were hidden from the public. The tunnels allowed staff to travel from one side of the park to the next, using colour coded pathways. It was also where the water pipes that fed into all the tanks across the entire park were fitted.

Dr. Fishnip remembered the secret tunnels from his time spent there, having been transported through them several times, and knew that one carefully chosen section – the staff canteen – was more than big enough to base his operations for the next stage of his despicable plans.

OFFICIAL PLANS FOLLOWING MY ESCAPE

by Dr. Fishnip Psc

1. Secretly takeover Aquaworld late at night *(when no staff members are present)*
2. Infiltrate underground tunnels *(and locate staff canteen)*
3. Unpack boxes *(Note: remember to bring scissors)*
4. Construct laboratory and factory *(but try do it quietly, just in case)*
5. Make x3 Robot Soldiers to defend me *(Note: Maybe call them 'Beat Bots' and install the 'Dance_2.0_upgrade' file, just in case I need some entertainment)*
6. Start construction of fish army *(then prepare for war!)*

12

COULD WE BE HEROES?

William raced through the woods, hot on the heels of the super-speedy Vanessa. He bounded, taking giant leaps, and it was only a few seconds before he found her.

"You can't just do that without warning me!" said a breathless William, seeing Vanessa kneeling on the floor. But Vanessa didn't answer immediately, and as William walked around her, he discovered she was beside an injured deer.

The deer wriggled in agony, kicking its long legs, and making a pained, whining noise that made William's hairs stand on end. A heavy branch had landed on the animal's back, trapping it underneath, and no matter how hard the deer tried to kick itself free, it just couldn't escape. Even worse, it seemed to be frightened by the freakishly giant animals that had arrived at the scene, perhaps assuming they'd come for their dinner.

"It's alright, we're not going to hurt you," reassured Vanessa, in a calm comforting voice.

"We need to try help it," William said.

"Can you lift the branch off?" asked Vanessa as she stroked the distressed animal.

"I could try, but that looks extremely heavy."

"William, have you *seen* the size of your muscles?"

William looked at his arms, the biceps protruding. He then looked down at his chiselled chest and toned eight-pack. "Wow. I'm absolutely ripped, aren't I?"

Vanessa growled. "William, STOP admiring yourself and help this deer. Right now!"

When Vanessa told you to do something, you tended to do it. She had a way with words and in her new wolf form, she was more than a little threatening too.

William grabbed the giant branch, gripping it tightly with his claws. He lifted it, expecting to have to use all his might, but to his surprise it was incredibly easy. Like picking up a twig! Gripping either end of the branch, William snapped it in two, then threw it off to the side. Both he and Vanessa then carefully helped the deer to its feet (or *hooves*, to be exact).

Vanessa assessed the injured animal as it stood unsteadily before her. She stroked its fur softly, hoping to calm it down. "It's a little bruised, but I think it's going to be okay," she said.

The deer looked at her, no longer scared now. It sniffed, and appeared to be inspecting Vanessa, trying to understand the strange creature that had helped to save its life. Then, it stuck out its pink tongue and licked Vanessa's face up and down.

"I think it's saying thank you," laughed William.

After delivering a sloppy kiss, the deer grunted, then trotted away in a sprightly fashion, practically skipping with delight. William and Vanessa looked to each other, thrilled to have saved the animal, but equally astonished at what they'd just achieved.

"When you heard that deer in pain, how did you know exactly where to go?" questioned William.

"I could hear it as if it was right by me. And I could sense exactly where it was. It's hard to explain, but I just knew how to find it, like some sort of noise activated GPS."

"And I'm guessing you couldn't do that before? Like, when you were a normal human?"

Vanessa shook her head. "And I'm also guessing that display of strength wasn't typical either, William? I mean, you were a bit of a weakling before today, if I'm being completely honest."

William inspected his scaly green hands and clenched them together into fists. "No, that was... surprising to me too, actually."

Then he looked at Vanessa, suddenly realising what

she'd said, and feeling a little offended by it. "Wait, I wasn't *that* weedy, was I? I always thought I had pretty big muscles for a kid!" William flexed his arms, admiring himself again.

Vanessa shook her head and put her hands on his shoulders. "But don't you realise, William? We don't have to worry about who we were *before*. Thanks to that green alien goo, now we're incredible!"

William nodded, but then thought for a moment, comprehending the events of the last 24 hours. He scratched his scaly bonce. "Have we got... *superpowers*?"

"Um... I mean, I think so? If that's what you want to call it."

"But that's bonkers. I can't believe this is even happening?!"

"I'm just hoping the formula wears off soon... I'm not entirely sure how I'll explain my new appearance to my parents."

"Yeah... And my stepmother would probably sling me in a cage given the chance. Put me in the basement too. Or dump me in the river outside our home."

"William, you don't think this transformation is permanent, do you?"

William and Vanessa hadn't considered the possibility of this being a long-term effect, and it was starting to sink in that maybe they needed to go back to their original plan of tracking down the man responsible, in order to get answers, and hopefully a way to reverse this at the same time.

"El Presto will surely know what to do," said William confidently.

Vanessa shook her head dismissively. "He's probably the only one that *does*, although from everything he's told us so far I get the feeling his line of work doesn't come with an 'undo' button. He might know how to make the impossible

possible, but can he ever put things back to what they were in the first place?"

"But we have to try, surely? What other choice do we have?"

Vanessa agreed. "Yeah, we should try. Question is, whereabouts in Cruz City is El Presto hiding right now?"

"I might have an idea," replied William. "Follow me."

13

THE MAGICIAN'S HIDEOUT

W hen a famous performer goes on tour, they'll often use a mammoth-sized bus to transport themselves and their team around in. This means they get to travel in comfort and luxury as they move from one venue to the next.

In a tour bus you might find a kitchen, multiple beds, a lounge, TVs, video game consoles, multi-coloured mood lighting and massive speaker systems that can blast music right through the whole interior. They're basically luxurious homes on wheels, and serve the purpose of keeping performers nice and fresh for their audience when they finally arrive at the venue they'll be performing at.

El Presto was no different, and his giant tour bus was ridiculously easy for William and Vanessa to find, because as they arrived in the theatre car park they saw the vast vehicle snaking across several parking spaces.

A neon pink EL PRESTO logo was splashed over the side of the bus, along with a giant picture of the magician's face emblazoned across the rear-end. With a twinkle in his eye, gleaming white teeth and pristinely perfect skin, the image could only be described as 'Photoshopped'. He looked at least 20 years younger, as if he'd gone back in time in Doctor Who's TARDIS and taken a photo of himself looking much more fresh-faced... Or found the strongest Snapchat 'youthify' filter possible and applied it multiple times. William and Vanessa had seen him up close and in detail, and there were certainly more than a few wrinkles and folds on his real-life face.

William knocked on the door to the bus and after a moment the hydraulics kicked in and it opened with a burst of air.

SSSSHHHHHHHHHHHHHH.

Emerging from the doorway was a portly bus driver, who was – according to a name badge, pinned to his left breast pocket – named Victor Ruddle. Victor was short, with a big round belly and a straggly overgrown beard. He looked like Santa's less successful brother, and cared so little about his appearance you wouldn't be surprised if he told you he'd never once owned a mirror.

William and Vanessa were still in their badly thought-out disguises but William's giant green feet and Vanessa's fur-covered hands were hard not to spot. And as Victor eyed them up, the duo were bracing themselves for a strong, perhaps even *horrified*, reaction. William thought it would likely be a combination of bewilderment and terror, accompanied by a deafening scream, and he covered his ears, preparing for the worst...

Surprisingly, that wasn't the reaction at all.

Victor simply spoke to them casually, with his grumbly, dull voice. It was such a non-reaction it was if William and Vanessa were an everyday occurrence. "I take it you've both met Mr. El Presto then?"

"Um, yes we have," replied a surprised Vanessa.

"Last night in fact," added William.

"Thought so," said Victor as he scratched his tummy, before digging into a family-sized bag of cheese and onion crisps. "That fella has a tendency for the weird and wonderful. Although I have to say, I've seen a lot of his experiments and not once have I seen him make a talking alligator or dog before."

William calmly corrected him. "Well, I'm a *crocodile*... I believe."

"And I'm a *wolf*," growled a less diplomatic Vanessa. "Not some kind of a dog, you big ninny."

"Alright, keep your fur on," replied Victor, not liking Vanessa's aggressive tone. "Listen, if you want to find him, he's in that hotel over there. Penthouse suite, right at the very top."

Victor pointed at a rather grand looking building across the other side of the car park. It was the *Hotel De Luxe*, the poshest, most expensive hotel in all of Cruz City. Legend has it, it was the first building to be constructed in the city, and the stone pillars and old-fashioned architecture showed that it was ancient.

"That building has over 14 floors, which is over 286 steps, as well as three elevators," said Vanessa, with a nugget of information that might've actually been useful for once.

"Oh crikey, how do we get in there without being seen?" asked William. He imagined each hotel floor to be like a video game level, where they'd have to use stealth skills to sneak past the various guests and workers. Only problem was, he and Vanessa stuck out like a sore thumb and would never make it past the hotel entrance. "I bet it's high security too!" said William, suddenly feeling a little dizzy with panic. "The police would be here in no time. We could get arrested!"

"Or I could attempt to climb up the wall. Can wolves do that kind of thing?" offered up Vanessa, trying to keep a cool head. "Or William, maybe you could use your amazing strength to shot-putt me onto his balcony?"

Victor stepped in. "Whoa, steady on. Though both of those sound absolutely valid ideas, young lady, especially considering the predicament you find yourselves in, perhaps it'll be easier if I just call his mobile phone and tell him you're here?"

"Ah yes," replied William, the panic inside him beginning to subside. "That definitely sounds a little bit more sensible."

"And safer too," added Vanessa.

E l Presto was lost for words. A rarity for this magician, who genuinely loved the sound of his own voice. For once, his voice was failing him.

"We need your help," said William, breaking the quiet in the room.

"Yes um... right, of course," replied El Presto, finally finding the ability to talk again.

The previous night, as El Presto had laid his head down on his ultra-luxury bamboo shredded memory foam pillow, he'd had a feeling of deep concern that something weird *might* happen to William and Vanessa, following their earlier exposure to the ooze... though in truth, as he considered all the possibilities, he'd had no idea that *this* would be the exact result.

See, through his studies, El Presto had discovered that the alien's green ooze was formulated from a variety of different secret sources, but one key component appeared to be a peculiar blend of animal DNA. In trying to manufacture his own version of the ooze in his lab, El Presto had taken it upon himself to visit every zoo across the country, collecting DNA from hundreds of different species.

After months of travelling, El Presto had returned home and begun to combine all the genetic information he'd collected. Eventually, after much testing (and many failed attempts) he was able to produce his own version of the very strange concoction. And through certain tweaks to the ingredients in the ooze, El Presto had found he could engineer it to do *exactly* what he needed it to, as long as it was only used in very small doses. For example, Fishnip had been subjected to only a very minuscule amount, barely a tea-spoon's worth... but the effects were clear to see.

Unfortunately, on that fateful night, William and Vanessa had been literally *drenched* in the stuff...

And as El Presto was turning back and forth in his bed, his mind doing cartwheels over the possibilities, he realised he'd made one *very big mistake...* He'd never tested to see what the effect would be if a *child* came into contact with the green ooze... but now the results were stood right before him.

El Presto had met William and Vanessa in the lobby of the hotel and managed to sneak them up to his penthouse suite without anyone seeing them. Well, apart from one of the hotel porters who had taken a curious glance towards the trio, but El Presto easily brushed him away by telling him they were "on their way to an exclusive celebrity-only costume party."

El Presto's suite took up the entire top floor of the hotel and was so big you could comfortably live in it for the rest of your life. It had 2 bathrooms, 3 bedrooms, a bar, the biggest flatscreen TV they'd ever seen, and a jacuzzi.

As William walked through the suite in a state of awe, he couldn't help but see the view over Cruz City. It was magnificent, and they were so high that William thought he could even see the floodlights of Foghorn High if he squinted.

Vanessa laid across the largest sofa whilst El Presto poured them both a glass of milk in his mini kitchen. "I have to say," said El Presto as he looked over at William and Vanessa, "that this is quite possibly the most amazing thing I've ever done." Vanessa was less than impressed and growled back at El Presto in annoyance.

"You do realise you've changed our lives forever? We're stuck like this!" she barked.

"Not exactly," replied El Presto as he handed Vanessa her milk, spilling a little bit on her fur-covered legs. Adrenaline was pumping through his body and he was struggling to maintain his excitement at his guest's shocking transformation. "There might be a way to reverse this, but I'll need some time to experiment in order to concoct the antidote for you."

"How much time?" demanded Vanessa. But before El Presto could come up with an answer, he was distracted by a Breaking News Report on the TV.

They all huddled around the large flatscreen, and El Presto grabbed the remote and turned up the volume so they could hear the reporter speak on CRUZ NEWS 24-7.

'WE HAVE A BREAKING REPORT THAT A LARGE FISH-HEADED ROBOT HAS BEEN BROADCASTING TERRIFYING THREATS AGAINST THE PEOPLE OF CRUZ CITY. POLICE ARE CURRENTLY TRYING TO IDENTIFY HIS WHEREABOUTS AND ARE ASSESSING THE POTENTIAL DANGER THE CITY MAY BE IN. OUR SOURCES TELL US THAT THIS VILLAIN GOES BY THE NAME OF DR. FISHNIP AND THAT HE IS LIKELY THE ESCAPEE FROM THE RECENT EL PRESTO STAGE PERFORMANCE... OUR SOURCES AREN'T CURRENTLY SURE WHAT HE'S A DOCTOR OF EXACTLY, BUT WE'LL CONTINUE TO UPDATE YOU AS WE LEARN MORE ABOUT THIS UNFOLDING INCIDENT... BUT THE BIG QUESTION REMAINS, WHO OR WHAT WILL SAVE US NOW?'

El Presto's face was as white as a sheet.

"What's wrong Mr. Presto?" asked William. El Presto turned away, grabbed Vanessa's glass of milk and drank it one gulp.

"Hey!" shouted Vanessa, as El Presto wiped the froth from his mouth.

"I'm sorry Vanessa," he replied, "but my throat suddenly dried up when I realised what was happening."

"You know what Fishnip's plan is, don't you?" said Vanessa, jumping to her feet. She loomed tall over El Presto and William couldn't help but think how imposing she was now.

El Presto nodded, then explained: "Dr. Fishnip said on-stage that he wanted payback for the way we've treated his species, and with my magic ooze he could transform *hundreds* of fish! We could have a revolution on our hands... Who knows what they could do?"

William was confused. "But they're only *fish*, aren't they?"

El Presto blew out his cheeks, his whole demeanour suddenly changing. This was no longer the confident and exuberant El Presto that the children were used to. Now, with his shoulders slumped and sweat pouring down his face, he looked helpless and panicked.

"Yes, but if Dr. Fishnip can do all this on his *own*, imagine what hundreds and hundreds of highly intelligent fish could do? Fishnip is a genius, don't you see? If he manages to turn the aquatic world against us, it could be World War 3!"

"But how do we stop him, when we don't even know where he is?" asked Vanessa.

El Presto tapped his chin as he thought to himself. Then, it came to him in a flash: "I know where he is... It's obvious!"

William realised now too. "He's at Aquaworld, isn't he?"

"Of course," said Vanessa. "They've got 12 sharks, 7 whales, 39 penguins, 28 dolphins, 425 tropical fish, 309 marine fish. They've also got 82 cold-water fish – which is the same type of fish as Dr. Fishnip. At last count there were over 200 different species in the park."

El Presto paced around the room, as William and Vanessa watched on. William scratched his head, thinking. He was also reminded again of his bald head, which was still incredibly irritating. Maybe El Presto could use his science to grow his hair back again? Would that look weird? William realised he was getting distracted by some largely unimportant questions, but suddenly something hit him... It was Vanessa, punching him in the arm to get his attention.

"I've got an idea" she said excitedly, as William rubbed his sore arm. "The news reporter lady on TV, asked 'who will save us now'? Well, with your strength and my speed and super-hearing we could really be something special. Don't you see? We've got superpowers, and Cruz City needs superheroes right now."

William's eyes opened wide. Vanessa was right. *Again*! Only there was one problem... "The whole world will see us and if that happens there might not be any way to go back to the way things were? Back to our normal life?"

Vanessa shook her head. "No, but if we don't do this, Fishnip could change the world anyway. And then what? No more fish and chips? No more killer shark movies? No more fish-tanks in doctors' surgeries?"

El Presto had heard the entirety of the conversation and knew that what they were saying was true. He couldn't bear to think of what the future might hold, considering it was his own crackpot experiments that had started all this. Everything had been a result of *his* tinkering, interfering with science in a way that was completely unnecessary, and done only for selfish reasons. (So he could get *extremely* rich.)

"You'll need costumes" said El Presto, stepping between William and Vanessa. "And I know exactly the person to sort you out." El Presto turned and shouted towards one of the closed doors in the suite. "Mother! Wake up, I need you!"

After a brief moment, the door opened and out stepped a short elderly lady, rubbing her tired eyes. Curly grey hair, emerald night-dress, and an eye mask pulled up over her forehead, she didn't look too pleased to be woken up.

"My goodness, what's all the racket about, Peter?"

William and Vanessa looked at El Presto, and together they mouthed "Peter?"

El Presto raised his eyebrows, his face flushed beetroot red. "Mum, I told you not to call me that in public. Remember my stage name!"

The little woman looked to William and Vanessa but – like Victor before her – didn't seem particularly surprised by their appearance. "Oh, Peter my silly little poppet, I keep telling you..." she said in a sweet voice, "you've got to stop with your animal experiments. I warned you something bad like this would happen with that fish of yours, didn't I?"

El Presto tilted his head and nodded, like a naughty child being told off, then grabbed his slow-moving mother by the shoulders and manoeuvred her towards his guests. "I know, and I'll fix things. This is all my fault, I get it, but I need everyone to work together to help me to stop Fishnip." He turned to his mother; it was clear he was desperate.

"From you, my marvellous mother, I need your skills at designing costumes, like the ones you make for me on-stage. They need to be special, heroic, tight-fitting. You know, like all those comic-book movies?"

El Presto's mother looked at William and Vanessa, scanning them up and down as if virtually taking their measurements with her eyes. "Fine, fine. But what are you calling them?" she asked.

"Ah, good question," replied El Presto. "What shall we call you both? Superheroes need super names!"

William and Vanessa thought for a minute, having not really considered this type of question coming up today, and what their answer might be if they were put on the spot. "How about Croc-Boy?" suggested William.

"No," replied Vanessa. "That sounds too much like you're a kid."

William was surprised. *But I am a kid!* he thought to himself.

Over the next five minutes, they all worked on name suggestions for him. Some were, to be fair, quite decent and well worth considering. Others were entirely embarrassing, and William found himself wincing at the thought of being called something like *The Greeny*.

Here's some of the names that were put forward:

- *The Snout.*
- *Scales.*
- *The Amazing Crocodile.*
- *Snappy.*
- *Crocodilicus.*
- *Crocky-Croc.*
- *The Crockster.*
- *Leatherskin.*
- *Child-odile.*
- *Green-Machine.*
- *The Hatchling.*
- *Crocodile-Kid.*

- *Chompy.*
- *Captain Crockadilly,*
- *Swamp Titan.*
- *The Creature of Cruz City.*
- *Crockers.*

William patiently waited for them to finish their suggestions before taking a breath and making a further one of his own: "How about... CROC-MAN?"

Everyone looked around at each other, considering the name. Then, they smiled, nodding vigorously.

"I like that one a lot, my dear," exclaimed El Presto's mother. El Presto fist-bumped Croc-Man, looking like a proud father trying too hard to be cool.

Then William turned to his friend. "How about you, Vanessa? Do you have any ideas for what you could be called?"

Vanessa thought for a second, lowering her head so those cogs in her brain could whir. Then it came to her, and of course it was inevitable.

She would choose the name: **WOLF-GIRL**.

14

DANCE OFF

"**O**kay, I'm just going to come out and say it..." screamed Wolf-Girl (a.k.a. Vanessa). "We. Look. Totally. AWESOME."

They were standing outside a large gift-shop outside the main entrance to Aquaworld, admiring their reflections in the tall, immaculately cleaned windows.

Croc-Man (a.k.a. William) nodded enthusiastically. "We're like proper superheroes now, aren't we?"

Croc-Man's super-suit was blue, covering most of his muscular body. He had matching blue boots too, with heavy, clumpy heels that made him look even taller. A large white *C* illuminated his chest.

Wolf Girl's super-suit was pink, with a yellow V that ran from her neck to her stomach. She had matching yellow gloves, black glittery boots and that same pink bow in her hair (refusing to leave El Presto's suite without it). Her suit was purposely designed by Mum Presto to be skin-tight, so it'd be extra *aerodynamic*, meaning there'd be minimal resistance from the air when she travelled at super-high speed. She puffed out her chest, looking incredibly heroic.

"You know what I think makes us look *extra* amazing though?" asked Croc-Man.

"The bandanas," replied Wolf-Girl, knowing exactly what he was going to say.

They both wore bandanas which wrapped around their heads, and as mega-fans of the Teenage Mutant Ninja Turtles, it was pretty much the most exciting thing that had happened today. Well, aside from them having transformed into giant animal superheroes, obviously.

"Mum Presto absolutely nailed these didn't she?" said Croc-Man.

Wolf-Girl nodded and looked at her best friend with a warm smile. "You know, *your* mother would've been so proud to see you right now, William."

Will – Um, *Croc-Man* – looked down with sadness for a moment. His mum had been a bit of a comic book nerd and had introduced William to a lot of the greats at a very young age. From the web-slinging heroics of Spider-Man, to the Detectiving of Batman and Robin, he'd read them all. Many of the comic books he owned had been inherited from his mum, and William made a point to try and read one every night before he fell asleep. It was kind of a ritual, that had become so important to his bedtime routine he'd now struggle to sleep without doing it.

William thought about his father, too, who was barely ever around. He'd missed every single one of William's school plays, his karate tournament, his piano recital, and when his Sunday football team won the Junior cup. Now he wouldn't be here to witness his son's bravest feat, either. But maybe that was a good thing? He'd surely try to talk William out of it if he knew what his son was about to do.

"So, we know Dr. Fishnip has plans to turn those fish into his soldiers... but what we don't yet know is what awaits us on the other side of these gates," assessed Wolf-Girl.

"No," replied Croc-Man. "But we do know that we have the element of surprise here, and we can use that to our advantage."

"Definitely," agreed Wolf-Girl, as they both began to climb over the tall metal gates.

Landing on the other side, the place looked deserted. Fortunately, the empty shops, stalls and attractions were also a clear sign that visitors had managed to safely escape before Dr. Fishnip had been able to capture or injure anyone.

Walking through the entrance to the park, and along the long stretch of wooden planks that made up the boardwalk, Croc-Man and Wolf-Girl headed towards the collection of buildings and outside tanks that housed the fish.

It felt eerily quiet.

Almost too quiet...

Croc-Man (in William form) had visited this place many times in his life and had always thought it would be cool to have the park all to himself, and not have to deal with the swarms of guests and lengthy queues. But something about the emptiness he was seeing right now made it feel more like a ghost town, and it was starting to really creep him out.

Reaching the main square, they stopped to look at the sign that featured an oversized park map.

"Where do you think he's hiding?" asked Croc-Man.

Wolf-Girl ran her finger along the map, seeing the penguin pool, shark lagoon, 4-D cinema and other exciting places of interest. She almost wished she wasn't here to fight Dr. Fishnip and could instead enjoy any one of the numerous attractions.

"He could be here? That's the biggest building in the park," said Vanessa as she pointed to the Indoor Submarine Wreck walkthrough exhibit.

GZZZZZRRTTTT!

Suddenly, a huge cinema-sized screen flashed on behind them. They spun around and were surprised to see Fishnip, in all his cybernetic glory, being filmed live from somewhere deep within the park. Dr. Fishnip was hyperactively stomping back and forth, water almost tipping out of his bowl, clearly excited to see his guests. The screen was so big, he looked about 30 feet tall.

"Well isn't this very strange?" he said, his metal thumbs twiddling. "I thought that someone might come and try stop me. The *police* maybe, or even the *army*. But you two? How very unexpected!"

"You need to stop what you're doing!" bellowed Croc-Man. The 's' in 'stop' almost had a hiss to it.

"Yeah," snarled Wolf-Girl, "and if you don't, we're going to find you and squish you!"

Surprised, Croc-Man turned to Wolf-Girl. "We didn't agree to squishing, did we?" he whispered.

"Sorry," replied Wolf-Girl. "I got a little bit excited. No squishing, I promise."

"I'm not scared of your threats, you fools!" smiled Dr. Fishnip wickedly. "My titanium body was made to withstand extreme impacts, pressures and temperatures. You couldn't even *scratch me*, you imbeciles."

Vanessa had already heard enough. "Alright, enough of the insults, just tell us what you want!"

Dr. Fishnip swam around buoyantly in his little bowl, keen to share his masterplan. "Well..." he started, "Aquaworld is full of my brothers and sisters. And you know what? We're *fed up*. Fed up of being kept in tanks to amuse other people, fed up of being cooked, and fed up of being eaten by greedy humans."

Croc-Man and Wolf-Girl looked at each other, finding it hard not to sympathise with Fishnip's anger in some small way.

"So, I realised," said Dr. Fishnip, "that the only way to change things, was to allow my aquatic pals to group together and fight back. Thus, I will be using El Presto's green ooze to give them a *voice*, to give them *power*, to give them *freedom*!"

The little fish corkscrewed in his tank, before looping his attention back towards the camera filming him. He wasn't finished with his diabolical speech just yet.

"And we will fight: *Fish vs. Humans...* And we – the aquatic creatures of this world – will be victorious!"

He tried his hardest to perform a wickedly deep evil-villain laugh, but his very limited fishy vocal cords meant it sounded more like a chipmunk on helium.

Then Dr. Fishnip stomped away from the camera, revealing something that sent a *chill* through both Croc-Man and Wolf-Girl... A trio of *robots* – or BEAT BOTS to give them their proper names – were carefully removing fish from tanks, putting them on conveyor belts, and one-at-a-time, dousing them with green droplets from a canister of El Presto's ooze. It was like a factory, but rather than making something normal like fast cars, chocolate biscuits or cuddly toys, it was making SUPER-FISH.

The TV suddenly blinked off, and Fishnip was gone. Immediately everything was quiet again, and Croc-Man and Wolf-Girl were left trying to understand what they'd just seen and heard.

"That single canister of ooze is all he's got for now, and that won't last him long," said Wolf-Girl as she punched her hand into her palm aggressively. "We need to get to Fishnip and stop him before he can get his hands on any more of the stuff."

Croc-Man started stretching his arms, looking like he was warming up for a P.E. lesson. "I agree, let's go put an end to this now."

Croc-Man and Wolf-Girl then walked in what felt like one of those cool slow-motion scenes from stylish Holly-wood action films. If this was indeed a movie, then a dramatic orchestra, with BIG heavy drumbeats would be blasting out. This was *their* moment. They were heroes now, and they were going to save the day!

But suddenly, there was a clanking of metal, the winding of gears and cogs, and the hissing sound of air being released... Croc-Man and Wolf-Girl whirled round in surprise, to see the trio of Beat Bots dropping from the sky above, and landing before them.

The big clunky robots weren't the most elegantly designed – it looked as if Fishnip had built them by piling different sized metal boxes on top of each other and gluing them together. Their snake-like arms were made from large bendable pipes, and they had flashing red lightbulbs for eyes. Despite all that, the sheer scale of them made them *terrifying*, and they now had our heroes trapped.

Uh-oh...

"Beat Bots assemble!" shouted the middle robot, before pressing a green PLAY button on his metal chest-plate.

BOOM, BOOM, BOOM!

Loud electronic pop music was now playing from speakers built into each of the Beat Bots. The tune was so catchy, Wolf-Girl couldn't help but tap her foot along to it. Then, like a team of well-rehearsed dancers, the Beat Bots all began to move in tandem. Arms swinging, heads bobbing, bodies swaying, legs kicking... they were in total synchronisation.

"Are they... Um... *dancing*?" exclaimed Wolf-Girl, taken aback. And they *were* – in an amazing routine that it was almost impossible not to be enthralled by.

"I guess if this evil villain thing doesn't work out, maybe Dr. Fishnip has a career in dance choreography?" muttered Croc-Man.

With each dance step, the Beat Bots drew closer to Croc-Man and Wolf-Girl. And as the pop song hit its chorus, Croc-Man and Wolf-Girl had found themselves so distracted that when a break-dancing routine ended with the Beat Bots collectively throwing an almighty PUNCH, they were completely unprepared for it.

BOOOOOOOOOOOOOOOOSH!

Croc-Man and Wolf-Girl flew through the air, slamming with force into the Reptile House.

SMACK!

They both slid down the building, eventually landing back on the hard ground again.

"Ow, that really hurt!" said Wolf-Girl, rubbing her sore back.

Croc-Man peeled himself up from the floor, wiping off the dust and rubble. "We allowed ourselves to be distracted. We can't let that happen again, or we'll be toast" he said, annoyed and slightly achy.

"I agree. So, we need a plan," replied Wolf-Girl as she straightened out her bandana. "And I think I know exactly what to do."

The Beat Bots were now on their backs, windmilling on the floor like a skilful breakdancing crew. Any talent-show judge would've given them the golden buzzer already, they were *that good*. However, Wolf-Girl knew from her years of expensive dance classes that she had her own secret weapon against these villainous mechanical performers. She stood before the trio, with Croc-Man now nowhere to be seen, and began to demonstrate a most beautiful balletic performance. She pirouetted in a hypnotic fashion, and it wasn't long before she was having exactly the effect she wanted...

The Beat Bots were entranced.

If there was one thing William was never great at it was swimming. But Vanessa had told him "humans can on average swim at a speed of 4 miles per hour. Whereas a crocodile can swim at an average of 18 miles per hour, which is over four times faster... But you're not an *average* crocodile." She was right, now he was Croc-Man he could feel the super-strength in his scaly legs, which he was confident would give him even more kicking power.

With the Beat Bots distracted, Croc-Man slipped into one of the large underwater tanks and began to swim back and forth, faster and faster, kicking harder and harder. His legs were a blur, and all the motion was beginning to create ripples and waves in the water.

Wolf-Girl continued to dance, performing beautifully infront of the Beat Bots. They were so enthralled that they'd failed to notice *the giant wave* tumbling right towards them!

SPLOOOOOOOOSH!

The Beat Bots were drenched... Water dripped down their shiny surfaces, and within seconds they knew something was wrong.

Suddenly their electronics began to crackle, and then their circuit-boards fried, as flashes of electricity wriggled like snakes over them. .

Wolf-Girl and Croc-Man stood a safe distance away and watched their evil foes as their internal systems buzzed and popped. A jolly tune started to chime from their speakers, like the sound a computer makes when it shuts down, and finally they were finished. The Beat Bots crumpled to the floor in a heap, enveloped in black smoke, and it was quiet again.

"We did it!" screamed Wolf-Girl excitedly. She pirouetted one last time in celebration.

"Now, let's go stop Dr. Fishnip," said Croc-Man. triumphantly.

Vanessa smiled. "Let's do it super-friend."

Croc-Man and Vanessa hurriedly explored the park. Behind every door they expected to see Dr. Fishnip, or another Beat Bot, or maybe even one of the transformed fish-soldiers. They discussed what might be waiting for them next - perhaps a highly intelligent man-eating shark? Or a killer whale with a desire to actually _kill_?

Wolf-Girl reminded Croc-Man that neither of those things were actually fish, but it was clear Fishnip wasn't concerned with technicalities - the only thing that appeared to matter was seeing through his despicable plans using whatever sea creature was at his disposal.

And the more Croc-Man thought about it, the more it scared him... Fighting some dancing robots was one thing, but he wasn't sure he was prepared for what else Dr. Fishnip had in store.

The weird thing was, wherever they went, Fishnip wasn't there. The place seemed deserted, and the villain was nowhere to be seen...

Confused, Croc-Man and Wolf-Girl took a seat on one of the park benches. It creaked and almost snapped from their combined weight.

Wolf-Girl shook her head, not understanding their predicament. "I don't get it," she said, "where could he have gone?"

Suddenly, Wolf-Girl had a dreadful thought. "What if he was *never* here... Or he was only here briefly... I mean, we both just managed to distract his Beat Bots, correct?"

Croc-Man nodded; not quite sure he knew where this line of thought was going yet. Wolf-Girl continued, "so, what if he's played us at our *own game*? What if *all of this* was just a distraction Fishnip made to get us here?"

Croc-Man was confused. "But if he's not here, where could he possibly be?"

Then, after a second of pondering, their eyes lit up, as they both realised the dreadful answer...

"El Presto's hotel!"

15

PLOT TWIST!

The media and police had already begun to gather around the hotel as Croc-Man and Wolf-Girl arrived. Blinking emergency lights, flashing cameras and the noise of general panic felt quite daunting for the superheroes, and when the attention was turned on them it took them both by surprise.

Though they both now *appeared* very different on the *outside*, on the *inside* they were still just children, and they'd have been lying if they'd said they weren't just the slightest bit terrified. After all, a typical day for them didn't usually involve fighting dancing robots or rescuing a world-famous magician from a maniacal talking fish.

It was becoming evident that Dr. Fishnip enjoyed being the centre of attention, so it was of no surprise that he'd announced his capture of El Presto, and his subsequent interrogation, with a YouTube livestream.

Crowds were now beginning to gather in their masses, fearing for the safety of the beloved magician, and news channels were broadcasting the event worldwide. If Croc-Man and Wolf-Girl thought they'd be able to sneak in without being seen, then that plan was about to change as they were about to be revealed... *to the world.*

"Ready?" asked Croc-Man.

"Ready," confirmed Wolf-Girl confidently.

As the pair walked triumphantly towards the front entrance of the building there were cries of 'Oooh' and 'Aaaah' from the crowd, who were all filming from their camera-phones. Shoulder-mounted news station cameras pointed at their faces, microphones were thrust at them with questions like 'Are you here to save El Presto?' and 'Are you the good guys or the bad guys?' Croc-Man and Wolf-Girl didn't answer, but as they moved through the throngs of people, they realised the mood was quickly changing.

"Are they booing us?" whispered Croc-Man, concerned at the reaction they were getting.

Wolf-Girl knew the truth though, her super hearing picking up every-last detail. "No, they're cheering us."

And she was right; there was clapping, whistles, and shouts of 'save El Presto,' and 'we love you, strange super-animal things!' Croc-Man wanted to correct them and announce their real super-names, but now wasn't the time to pause...

"Clear the way!" shouted one moustachioed police officer, as Croc-Man and Wolf-Girl walked through the front doors to the hotel. They entered the large and expensive looking lobby and paused to work out the fastest route to the penthouse suite.

When he was younger, Croc-Man (as William obviously) had once had dinner in the hotel's upmarket restaurant with his mother and father and had always dreamed of eating here again. His mother got sick soon after, so sadly he never got the chance to return, but now with all the delicious smells of food wafting through the lobby, the memories were starting to flood back.

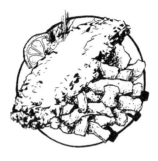

He remembered the fish and beer-battered chips, and the scrummy Eton Mess he'd followed up with for dessert. It was the nicest meal he'd ever had, and he could still recall today how crunchy the meringue was and how deliciously sweet the strawberries had tasted.

He'd assumed, at that young age, that he'd get to come back sooner, and sample even more delicious items from the menu, being that it was his parents' favourite place to eat in the city. However, he hadn't expected to walk back through the hotel doors in the form of a newly-famous muscle-bound crocodile.

"Are you okay?" asked Wolf-Girl, seeing Croc-Man staring at a framed picture of a delicious-looking Eton Mess dessert. Croc-Man explained his memory to his friend, but he didn't want her to think he wasn't prepared for the difficult challenge they were about to face.

"Honestly, I'm great," he replied. "Now let's go save El Presto and Cruz City."

16

THE FIN-ALE

DING... DING... DING... DING... DING... DING...
The elevator chimed every time it passed another floor. They were getting higher and higher and Croc-Man was taking big deep breaths, clearly nervous. With her super-hearing power, Wolf-Girl could hear his heart thumping fast in his chest.

"It'll be alright," she said, reassuring him. "As long as we work together, and don't do anything silly, we can beat Dr. Fishnip."

"But... we're just kids," said Croc-Man, feeling apprehensive.

"We aren't *just* kids," Wolf-Girl said, shaking her head. "That's not who we are anymore. Just look at us both!"

Croc-Man considered their transformation, and that there was probably nothing else like them on the planet.

"I guess," Croc-Man replied. "I mean, you could probably say we're... *special*?"

Wolf-Girl laughed, "yeah okay, fine. We're *special*."

"I mean, you were always spe..."

"Steady on," she said, interrupting him. "Don't overdo it

now." Wolf-Girl grabbed hold of his hand, and they both smiled.

She listened for his heartbeat. It was now a little slower.

Croc-Man and Wolf-Girl stepped out of the elevator, right into the penthouse suite. During the remaining ride to the top of the building, they'd tried to work out a plan of attack, to foil Dr. Fishnip's despicable plans. But they soon came to the conclusion that due to the unpredictable nature of Fishnip's actions so far, it was almost impossible to second-guess what might await them when the doors opened. There was a chance he might not even be there at all, and this might be yet another distraction.

What they *did* see was El Presto and his mother, sat on chairs and tied back-to-back with a thick rope. Their mouths were gagged and any attempts to scream sounded more like '*mmphhmmpphllmmpfftttmm*'...

"Are you okay?" asked Croc-Man.

El Presto and his mother shook their heads rapidly, eyes wide open and a look of terror on their faces... *Clearly something was wrong...*

Suddenly, from behind a stone pillar, emerged their captor, Dr. Fishnip. He had a mean smirk on his little orange face. "Welcome Croc-Man and Wolf-Girl, or should I say *children*?"

Croc-Man and Wolf-Girl turned to one another, realising their secret identities might not be so secret after all. As they quickly considered the ramifications of this news, Fishnip swam back and forth in his fishbowl, his robot body following him in total synchronicity.

His metallic hands clinked and scraped as he rubbed them together in glee. "I knew, when you both landed in the puddle of ooze in the alleyway, that it'd result in some sort of EXTRAORDINARY transformation... And I've been truly excited for your arrival in the flesh ever since. Hahaha!" Fishnip's malevolent laugh was much better this time, clearly he'd been practicing since his last attempt.

"One thing I don't understand..." said Wolf-Girl as she stood in a superhero-pose, hoping to physically express to Dr. Fishnip how powerful she now was in this form, "how did you find out about us before anyone else? The dancing robots... They were a trap, right?"

"Ah yes... My beautiful Beat Bots," said Fishnip, far too pleased with himself. "I'm guessing you defeated them? I have to say, I am impressed. *Most* impressed!"

It was hard to tell if he *was* genuinely impressed, or just very sarcastic.

"Answer my question!" demanded Wolf-Girl, anger bubbling inside her.

"Slow down little one. Let me enjoy this moment of triumph," replied Dr. Fishnip, the sound of wickedness in his voice. He picked up an El Presto t-shirt – a piece of official merchandise available on www.elpresto.com for £19.99 plus delivery – and used it to wipe the condensation from his fishbowl.

"You see," he started, "all good super-villains need to be one step ahead of everyone else. And what kind of super-villain would I be without having a few spies dotted around in secret locations, informing me of all the goings on behind the scenes?"

Croc-Man looked confused.

Spies?

Suddenly, from the shadows, stepped Victor Ruddle, El Presto's tour-bus driver. He was pointing a large glowing laser gun at our superheroes and appeared to have a bit of an itchy trigger finger.

"He was working for you all along?" exclaimed Croc-Man.

"Yes, and he gave me all the intel I needed to setup the distraction and prepare for your arrival," grinned Fishnip. "And it seems like that stage of my plan worked... Now, all I have to do is extract the information I need from El Presto on where the rest of his ooze is stored. After that, you'll all be transported to my secret underground base, where you'll be held captive until the mayor of Cruz City agrees to release all aquatic animals back into their natural habitats."

Wolf-Girl was still trying to understand the extent of her powers, but the super-hearing was continuing to prove to be quite handy. So handy in fact, that she'd already sussed out that someone else was hiding in the room from simply hearing them breathe. Victor's arrival then, perhaps didn't quite have the same level of surprise as for her as it did for Croc-Man, and whilst Fishnip had been doing his evil villain monologuing, Wolf-Girl had repositioned herself around one of the wooden coffee tables.

Victor was a good bus driver, a fairly average spy, and an even worse henchman. His sole job was to keep his laser gun focused on Croc-Man and Wolf-Girl, never taking his eyes off the heroes unless instructed otherwise. The problem was, Victor was the type of person that could be distracted by anything. If he was having a conversation and a pigeon flew by the window, he'd immediately be drawn to the flapping bird. If he was cooking dinner and a phone beeped nearby, he'd go in search of it even if it wasn't his. He would sometimes even get distracted, mid-conversation, by his own bottom burps, or anyone else's for that matter. It really didn't take much.

Realising that Victor was no longer focused on her or Croc-Man, Wolf-Girl slammed the bottom of her foot into the coffee table, causing it to slide with great speed across the floor. It collided with Victor's legs, tripping him over and causing him to land splat on his tummy.

Croc-Man reacted instantly, snatching the laser gun away, whilst Wolf-Girl speedily wrapped one of the hotel towels around Victor's waist and hands, making it impossible for him to move.

Dr. Fishnip rolled his eyes, then followed with a long sigh. "You absolute nitwit, Victor."

Croc-Man now aimed the laser gun in Fishnip's direction. He glanced over to El Presto and his mother, still tied to the chairs. "You're both safe now. Let's get you out of here."

But Croc-Man suddenly felt uneasy, as Dr. Fishnip's cackling laugh rudely interrupted what was feeling like a real-life Marvel-style action scene.

"You do know that the weapon you're holding is just a toy, right?" said the mean fish, with a devious little smirk.

At first, Croc-Man thought Dr. Fishnip was creating *another* distraction. But as he gripped the handle, he knew something didn't feel right. He juggled the gun back and forth between his hands.

"He's lying, isn't he?" said Wolf-Girl.

But Fishnip was right, the gun was completely hollow. Croc-Man pulled the trigger, and it made a crackly ZAPPING noise and tiny LED lights flashed red and green.

Croc-Man hissed, annoyed and perhaps a little embarrassed too. He dropped the toy to the ground and stamped down, crushing it into little bits with his clawed foot.

"Enough games," said Croc-Man, stepping towards his opponent. "This ends now! Release El Presto and his mother and we'll hand you safely over to Cruz City police."

Wolf-Girl joined in. "And if you don't, you'll see exactly just how powerful we are. We'll put an end to this little charade, Dr. Fishnip, and ensure you're dumped in the middle of the ocean, so far away you'll never know the direction home."

But Dr. Fishnip wasn't even a little bit scared. "Ha! I don't think so. Because right now, in my secret underground base, my Beat Bots are readying the factory for my return. Once I have El Presto's magical ooze, I'll be using it to create my own unbeatable fishy army. We'll be truly unstoppable and unrelenting, and this city will finally be mine."

As he sat, restrained by ropes in the chair, the great El Presto felt a chill run up his spine. He truly feared Fishnip, so single-minded was the fish in his desire to cause chaos. But quite frankly, El Presto was also a little bit fed up with being tied up whilst this showdown was taking place right before him. He felt utterly powerless.

El Presto's status as a world-famous science-magician gave him the wonderful opportunity of being able to talk to lots of people. And he *loved* to talk. Unfortunately, it appeared that Dr. Fishnip had inherited this trait, and it was all becoming a little bit tiresome to listen to. El Presto was slowly concluding that perhaps he liked the sound of his *own* voice a little bit too much, and that maybe he should try listen to other people a little more. Especially when those people were saying things like "Don't engineer a secret ooze that has unpredictable and transformative effects on anyone or anything it comes into contact with."

Actually, it was mainly his own mother who had been saying this, and El Presto was now feeling extremely guilty for not having listened to her all along.

Whilst El Presto was listening to Dr. Fishnip spout his ridiculous nonsense, he noticed that the fish-bot was getting closer and closer to him... Fishnip appeared to be circling around the room, like someone presenting a lecture on a stage (perhaps another thing he'd picked up from El Presto?).

And what Dr. Fishnip should've considered at some point, within his almost impeccably precise preparations, was that if you want to restrain a skilled magician (with a side-line in escapology), it's probably advisable to use something stronger than rope. Especially if you're not going to use some kind of advanced knotting technique like a bowline, double fisherman or alpine butterfly.

Long before El Presto was known for his unique brand of science-magic tricks, he was an escape artist. His most well-known trick saw him being sealed in a padlocked and chained barrel and thrown out the side of an aeroplane thousands of feet above the Earth. As he plummeted to his apparent death, El Presto escaped the barrel, clipped on a parachute, and landed safely on the ground right in front of a watching audience.

So, that's a rather exhaustive way of saying that escaping from this chair was an absolute cinch for him. He was just waiting for the right time to spring his surprise on Dr. Fishnip...

Sensing that now was as good an opportunity as any, El Presto *leapt* from his chair. "Game over Fishnip!" he yelled courageously. But Fishnip's agile robot suit sensed the threat immediately, and swiftly dodged out of the way.

"Whoops," whimpered El Presto as he rushed past helplessly, missing Dr. Fishnip entirely. El Presto's momentum was so powerful that he couldn't stop himself, and instead of heroically tackling the villainous fish he found himself flying out through the open balcony doors, and right over the balcony railings. His arms windmilled as he plummeted.

"El Presto!!!" screamed Wolf-Girl, who wasn't quick enough to react.

El Presto's mother could only watch helplessly from her chair as her son disappeared from view.

There were shouts and shrieks from the crowd below, who had also witnessed El Presto's awful calamity. Wolf-Girl and Croc-Man felt numb, and truly disgusted by Dr. Fishnip's outward joy as he danced and roared with a vile laugh.

"You do realise that if he's dead, you won't know where his ooze is, right?" said Wolf-Girl, on the verge of tears.

Dr. Fishnip promptly stopped dancing, knowing she was right.

"Oh fiddlesticks!" he shouted.

Then, a little voice came from somewhere...

"Guys, I'm okay!"

"Wait... Is that El Presto?" asked Croc-Man, furrowing his scaly brow.

"No, it can't be..." replied Wolf-Girl in disbelief.

Fortunately, as he fell over the balcony's edge, El Presto

had managed to twist his body at the last minute, grabbing onto one of the metal railings. He was clinging for dear life, hanging high above the crowd below... but he was alive!

Phew...

El Presto's mother sighed the biggest sigh, knowing her precious son hadn't landed smack on the city streets below.

"I don't know how long I can hold on for!" shouted El Presto, who was gripping onto the rails so tightly his knuckles were turning white.

Dr. Fishnip realised he could use this sudden change of situation to his advantage though. "I can save you," the fishy fella said, "just so long as you tell me where I can get the rest of your secret formula."

"I'd never tell you that!" shouted back El Presto. "I'd rather die!"

"Well, my wondrous *previous* owner...", replied Fishnip, "I can see to that right away."

Dr. Fishnip began to walk over to El Presto, his metal feet clanging on the floor, ready to strike a final deathly blow. "If you don't want to tell me, I'm sure I can find out some other way... After all, I'm sure your lovely *mother* would be happy to share that information with me, if I asked her... *nicely*." Dr. Fishnip squinted his eyes and gave the most deliciously evil look to El Presto's mum. She was next on his hit-list, that was certain.

But Croc-Man and Wolf-Girl had heard enough.

No more talking. No more standing around. Time to do the thing they'd come here to do in the first place... *stop Dr. Fishnip*.

Wolf-Girl scanned the room, considering what options they had in order to foil him once and for all. She thought back to her new friendship with William... how they met, how alike they were, the things they'd enjoyed doing together in the brief time they'd been friends...

Then it came to her...

Tiddlywinks.

William and Vanessa were both champion Tiddlywinks players, and though to most it seemed like an entirely ridiculous sport to partake in, right now it was perhaps the best hope they had.

Wolf-Girl pointed at two plush leather sofas in front of them. One was a large three-seater, the other a single chair. She then glanced over to Croc-Man and whispered: "Tiddlywinks."

At first, Croc-Man was confused. He squinted, and quietly mouthed 'huh' at his fearless friend. Then she followed up with another word that might make more sense to him: "Squidger."

"What are you two whispering?" demanded Dr. Fishnip, clenching his fists tightly.

However, Croc-Man was no longer confused. He'd seen the large sofa in front of him, and finally understood the instruction.

And he knew it *might* just work.

"What are *you* going to do?" questioned Croc-Man, quiet as a mouse. Wolf-Girl grinned a toothy grin, then cheekily replied, "Just you watch, my bald friend."

"I've had enough. Stop your whispering, *children*!" screamed Dr. Fishnip, stomping towards them.

They both looked directly at the fish-bot and replied in tandem, "We aren't children."

"We're Croc-Man and Wolf-Girl!"

Together, they leapt into action.

Wolf-Girl whizzed straight at Fishnip, as fast as a bullet train. As she ran, everything around her felt like it was moving in slooooow-motion. Meanwhile, Croc-Man lifted the huge sofa high above his head, and with a cry of 'tiddly-winks!' smashed the sofa back down on the arm of the smaller one.

BOOOOOOOOOOOOM!

The power of this hit caused the second sofa to flick like a giant tiddlywink counter, right into the hard metal frame of the unsuspecting Dr. Fishnip.

SMASH!

The booming force resulted in the fishbowl instantly detaching from the neck of the robot's body.

WHOOOSH!

Mother Presto watched as the fishbowl flew through the air, right over her head, and in the split-second prior to it impacting and shattering on the floor, Wolf-Girl caught it! Then, with a balletic spin, she roundhouse kicked the robot suit straight over the balcony.

She heard it drop like a meteor, whistling through the air before crashing to the ground with an almighty BANG. That was then followed by a collective 'Ooooooooooh' from the crowd and TV crews watching below.

El Presto was still struggling to hold on to the metal bars, and as the robot suit had shot past, his grip had loosened even further. His fingers began to prise away one at a time, and he knew he was about to fall...

For a moment, El Presto considered the current predicament he'd found himself in, and how it was all rather ironic. He'd spent so much of his adult life in front of cameras, being watched by millions the world over, and now here he was, about to fall to his death live on TV and the Internet. And there was nothing he could do about it.

His fingers slipped...

He swiped at the air helplessly...

And as he felt himself drop...

He closed his eyes tightly...

Until suddenly, he felt something *grab* hold of him...

Snapping his eyes open, he saw a giant, scaly hand holding his wrist...

And he was no longer falling.

El Presto could barely hold back the tears...

Croc-Man had saved him!

The lean, green superhero gently lifted El Presto over the balcony railings, and back to safety.

"I thought I was a goner for sure," said El Presto, who was so overwhelmed he couldn't help but give his rescuer the biggest hug. It was hard to express how happy El Presto felt in that moment

El Presto held onto Croc-Man for what seemed like an eternity, thankful to be alive.

A few days ago, if little William had been told that he would be responsible for saving El Presto's life as he fell to his death from a tall building, he'd have laughed. But as he looked down at El Presto, he could see the famous magician was truly in awe of Croc-Man and Wolf-Girl. Thanks to them, he was still here, alive and well, and the world was no longer under threat from a talking robot-fish and his aquatic army.

17

BATTERED FISHNIP

Not long after the dust had settled, a crack team of animal welfare experts arrived to take possession of Dr. Fishnip. They locked his tank in a metal cage, securing it tightly with five chunky padlocks. With Fishnip's extraordinarily high IQ, they knew there was a chance he'd find a way to break out if they didn't take extra precautions.

As Dr. Fishnip was removed from the building by the army of trained experts, he looked back to Croc-Man and Wolf-Girl with malice in his eyes. "I'll return, and will take my revenge on you all. You've not heard the last of Dr. Fishnip, mark my words!"

Croc-Man and Wolf-Girl didn't care for his threats and didn't offer any response. They knew that would annoy Fishnip more than anything. As the goldfish was finally driven away in the back of a black, armour-plated van they couldn't help but smile and wave, knowing the citizens of Cruz City were safe once again.

"Thank you, Croc-Man and Wolf-Girl, I owe you everything," said El Presto, hugging them both tightly again, as they stood inside the penthouse suite.

"No problem Peter... Ummm, I mean El Presto," replied Wolf-Girl. "We're just glad you're safe."

El Presto rubbed his hands, still sore from hanging on to the rails for all that time. "It's okay, you can call me Peter," he said, smiling. "But more importantly, what can I do to repay you both?".

Croc-Man and Wolf-Girl looked to each other, considering their response carefully. Both of them shared the same thought, about the very normal school-children they'd been, only yesterday, and what a crazy 24 hours it had been. But it was clear that the answer to El Presto's question was actually right in front of him... *He needed to find a way to return the children to their normal selves.*

El Presto felt a pang of guilt. "I know I said I'd be able to make an antidote, but in truth it's not going to be easy. And it's going to take me some time, and lots and lots of trials and tests. But I know I can do it, William and Vanessa. One day, I will make you both human again, I promise."

Neither Croc-Man nor Wolf-Girl had had time to prepare themselves for the possibility of this being anything more than a brief transformation. How would they go to school? How would they tell their parents? How would they sleep in their beds which were clearly now far too small for them?

But they could tell that El Presto was being sincere, and that no matter what they had to trust in him. Really, they had no choice...

However he'd already proven he could make the impossible possible, so there was surely no need to doubt him now. And perhaps, it wasn't so bad being superheroes for the time-being anyway? If Cruz City needed heroes right now, and it surely did, then that would have to be them.

There was a knock at El Presto's front door.

"Come in!" said Mother Presto, fresh out of a nice warm bath and in her favourite silk pyjamas.

"We've brought this for your guests," said the hotel porter as he wheeled a food trolley into the room. On the trolley was a huge metal dome, and when it was lifted it revealed the biggest Eton Mess dessert anyone had ever seen.

"Holy strawberries!" shouted Croc-Man as he bounded over to the trolley, mouth salivating.

"This was made at the special request of your friend,"

said the smiling porter, leaving the room. Croc-Man turned back to Wolf-Girl and gave her a huge goofy smile. "Thank you so much," he said as he cuddled her tightly. "I can't *believe* you did all this for me."

Vanessa wiped a tear from her eye, finally letting the emotions of the past day settle in. "Well, I can't *believe* I'm a crime-fighting wolf with super-speed and super-hearing, but since meeting you I think I've realised that anything can happen. Even the strangest and weirdest of things..."

———

I t took a few days for Aquaworld to remove Fishnip's machinery from their park, but the TV coverage had drawn a great deal of interest in their attractions, resulting in a huge increase in customers. People were flowing through the gates, excited to not only see the battle-ground where the city's newest superheroes fought the powerful Beat Bots, but also to see the amazing sea-life situated within.

If anything, Fishnip's speeches about the plight of aquatic animals had very much changed the view of the public, and more people than ever were trying to help save the ocean now. When interviewed on a popular breakfast show, El Presto had said: "Though this might not have been part of Dr. Fishnip's plans, at least some good has come of everything that's happened." He went on to say that "Fishnip was probably swimming in his prison cell some-where, content in the knowledge that he'd somehow still made a difference for all his brothers and sisters."

———

Hilda, William's wickedly evil stepmother, told him in a very stern manner that he'd no longer be welcome in the house. She stood in the doorway, blocking his entrance, threatening him with the pointy end of a broom handle. What she hadn't accounted for, was that she was talking to a crocodile, and as Vanessa had told William previously, "crocodiles can basically kill and eat anything. That includes sharks and humans."

And although William would never dream of doing such a thing, he only had to open his mouth and display his 64 razor-sharp teeth for his stepmother to step aside. After that, she kept out of his way, and promised to never treat him badly again. She even bought him a brand new, custom-sized bed, and paid for the house to be modified to make it easier for him to walk through door frames.

William had received a video-call from his father to tell him that he'd seen the news story, and that he'd since put in a request to his bosses to return home. "I wish I could've been there, to see you in action," he told his son in amazement. He was barely able to comprehend the excitement of his son's transformation and apologised repeatedly for being away for so long.

William was pleased to hear from his father, but in truth he was also a little sad that it had taken the recent shocking events for his father to want to return to see him again.

Vanessa's parents had watched the drama of El Presto's rescue when it was broadcast live worldwide. At the time, they hadn't known that their daughter was the heroic Wolf-Girl, and honestly, how would they have done? It wasn't until she arrived home the following day and knocked on the front door that all was revealed. Vanessa's mother, Sally, almost fainted when she first saw her Vanessa, but quickly came around to the idea of her daughter being a superhero, even though the whole family had to be sworn to secrecy about her true identity.

Vanessa's parents couldn't have been prouder and following an exciting visit from the famous El Presto, were assured that Vanessa would one day return to her true form again. The magician vowed to work around the clock to create the antidote, and nobody doubted him. Vanessa's father, Adam, offered to home-school both her and William, until they were back in their original forms. But fortunately, it was almost the summer holidays, so they knew they had a few weeks to work out what they might do next...

———

A month later, the Headmaster at Foghorn High received a small brown envelope. Upon opening it, he found a cheque inside.

The first thing he saw was the *figure*, a number so whoppingly high that it was more money than the school could've ever needed. Next he saw the signature, clueing him into *exactly* who sent the money:

Peter E. Presto.

"Oh my," said the Headmaster, breaking into floods of tears. "This will change everything!"

Though nobody ever found out how much money had been donated exactly, it was evidently enough to completely renovate the entirety of the school, inside and out. In just a short amount of time, during the summer holidays, it'd been reinvented from a crumbling old mess of a structure to a spectacular building like something from a big budget Sci-Fi movie. Upon entering through the school gates, it was like being transported in a time machine, and they'd even re-built the sports hall and courts to an Olympic standard too.

It didn't take much to work out *how* the school had suddenly become so fortunate, considering El Presto owed his life to the superhero duo that once attended Foghorn High.

When El Presto began his studies on the complicated antidote and did the math on just how long it might take to create, he wanted to try find a more *immediate* way to say thank you to his friends. And so, a shiny brand-new school was his way of showing his appreciation.

He just had one request... the basketball team would no longer be called 'The Sharks.' From that moment forwards, they'd be known as 'The Crocodiles'.

18

THE TAIL END

T he sun was setting just over the city. The sky glowed a fiery orange. And Croc-Man and Wolf-Girl were stood atop the tallest skyscraper.

They looked out at the buildings below, at the vehicles that looked like tiny Hot Wheels, and the people that looked like marching ants.

"There's around 7,591,500 people in Cruz City," said Wolf-Girl, always prepared with a fact for any occasion.

"And we need to be able to protect all of them," replied Croc-Man.

Whilst he took in the spectacular sight of the city, he wondered for a moment how many others there might be out there, who were like him and Wolf-Girl. Children and adults who had always considered themselves to be distinctly average, and didn't quite know how special they really could be if they just believed in themselves...

Croc-Man then thought about the future and couldn't wait to see what thrilling adventures lay ahead for him and his best friend, even the more daunting and scary ones. He was reminded of his mum's saying: "life has many hurdles, you just need to learn how to jump over them," and he understood what that meant now more than ever. The past few days and weeks had been incredible, and he'd faced more challenges in that short time than at any other point in his life. But he'd managed to overcome them, to learn to be brave in the face of adversity, and he now no longer felt scared to face whatever came next.

Wolf-Girl walked around the roof, using her super-hearing to listen out for any signs of crime within the city. She closed her eyes in concentration, focusing on the cacophony of sound below. Then suddenly, her eyes snapped open, and she spun and looked towards the sky above. *Something* was travelling lightning fast through the clouds, seemingly coming right towards them both like a high-speed rocket.

"Is it a bird?" Wolf-Girl asked, now wishing she also had super-vision.

"No, I don't think I know any flying birds that are... *pink*?"

"Is it a plane?"

Croc-Man shook his head. "No, it's too small".

"Well, is it Superm..."

Croc-Man cut her off. "No, I think it's a... *flying pig*?!"

PHOOOOOOOOOOOM!

The pink blur suddenly landed with great force before them both, sending a shockwave of stones everywhere. Eyes wide in surprise, Croc-Man and Wolf-Girl looked at the mysterious figure as it stepped towards them.

As the dust settled, a deep voice spoke out: "I'm Super-Pig."

Then *he* revealed himself in full: a pig, bubblegum pink in colour, wearing a red bandana and a long cape that flowed and rustled behind him in the wind. He was more like a normal-sized pig, not of the same scale as Croc-Man and Wolf-Girl. But despite his diminutive height he stood strong and confidently, chest puffed out.

"Did you say Super-Pig?" enquired Croc-Man.

"Why yes, that is I. And I'm here to kindly ask for your assistance."

Super-Pig spoke in a deep British-sounding voice, standing boldly with his trotters on his waist. "I've travelled from a planet, most distant from here, to tell you that a strange alien being is on its way to attack Cruz City... and I don't think I can stop her alone... Will you assist me in my fight?"

Croc-Man and Wolf-Girl turned to one another, high-fived and stood in their most heroic poses, ready for action.

"Count us in!" shouted Croc-Man resolutely, looking like he could take on the world.

"Then the legend that I was foretold is true," replied Super-Pig boldly. "You really are the great saviours of man and animal kind and I very much look forward to fighting by your side, in what I am sure will be your toughest challenge yet."

But that's a story for another time.

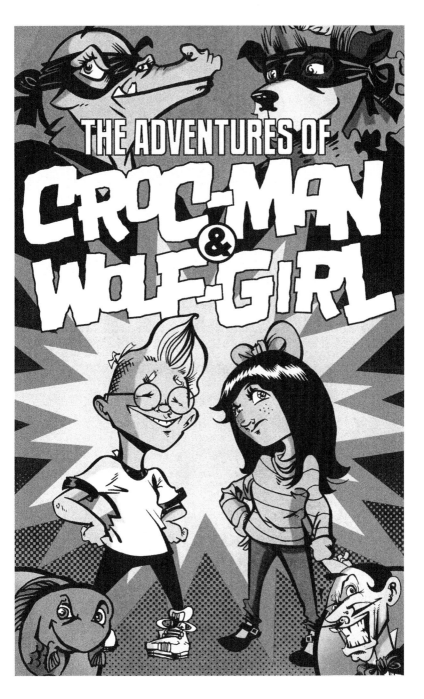

ABOUT THE AUTHORS

Riley Franklin is eleven-years-old and the mastermind behind Croc-Man and Wolf Girl. Mainly, Riley *loves* to draw, with countless characters and worlds created across his many art books piled across his bedroom floor.

Riley is also a big fan of video games, especially retro titles, and is always in his absolute element when he's designing impossible levels in *Mario Maker*. He dreams of one day having a career in which he can create his own video game worlds, which will undoubtedly be filled with even more of his incredible character designs.

At 4 years old, Riley was diagnosed with autism, but this has never stopped him. In fact, it's his very own superpower, giving him the most incredibly vivid imagination, a lot of which can be seen within the pages of this book. But of course there's so many more exciting characters and creations he can't wait to share with everyone!

Ben Franklin is a UK-based writer and filmmaker most well-known for his horror web-series Bloody Cuts (created with cofounder Anthony Melton), which has been critically praised for its use of practical makeup, Hollywood standard aesthetics and unconventional storytelling.

Ben's films for have been viewed over 50 million times, played at major festivals worldwide, and won awards - most notably a Webby in 2017. In 2020 Bloody Cuts also celebrated its 3rd year at Thorpe Park Resort's FRIGHT NIGHTS, where the franchise has become a major staple at one of the biggest theme parks in the UK.

Ben has a number of film and tv projects in development in the UK and US, and is also a co-producer of Crypt TV's THE BIRCH streaming series, produced exclusively for Facebook Watch.

Ben spends much of his spare time playing boardgames, video-games and producing retro 80's style music. He enjoys writing, having worked on film and television scripts for Hollywood studios, and secretly hopes that Croc-Man and Wolf-Girl might one day find their way into one of his scripts, and of course on to the big screen!

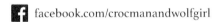 facebook.com/crocmanandwolfgirl

ABOUT THE ILLUSTRATOR

Karl Slominski is a dynamic analogue storyteller in the arenas of comic books and film, whose work focuses on universal, high-concept adventures featuring diverse characters from all walks of life. A graduate of the industry-renown KUBERT SCHOOL OF CARTOONING AND GRAPHIC ART, Slominski's work skews toward the traditional hand-crafted illustration and narrative methodology of the great comic-book forefathers that inspired him at a young age. His formative years spent within the rigours of art school and the road-tripped escapades of punk band follies have informed the electrically frenetic energy that occupies his body of work.

Clients have included Netflix, Ape Entertainment, 215Ink, Seraphemera Books, Z2 Comics, Glass Eye Pix, Fox Features, DC Comics, IDW Publishing, Sailor Records, and Trap Door Pictures.

His creator-owned graphic novella "TEETER TOPPLE" was hailed by Newsarama as "a work of true vision and heart, Karl Slominski wears his heart on his sleeve as does his book and us, the readers, are all the better for it." It is currently being developed for film through Limitless Entertainment.

Karl currently resides in Upstate New York as he finishes work on his upcoming all-ages graphic novel, EVERMORE FALLS.

twitter.com/KarlSlominski

instagram.com/karlslominski

RILEY'S ORIGINAL ARTWORK
(THAT INSPIRED THIS BOOK)

CROC-MAN

DR. FISHNIP

WOLF-GIRL

SUPER-PIG

ACKNOWLEDGEMENTS

From Ben...

Thank you to Emma for supporting Riley and I as we decided to go on this crazy adventure of writing a children's book. You've read this book numerous times, listened to us perform it, and always pushed us to do more and see it through to completion. We simply couldn't have done it without you! Thank you also to my darling Eloise for always being there for your big brother, and for always willingly throwing in great ideas when we needed them the most.

Thanks to my parents, Caroline and Roy, to my brother Jonny and my sisters Christabel and Melissa, all of whom have read, reported back, and helped to shape this book into what it now is. Thanks also to my wonderful extended family - Sharon, Natalie and each and every person that took the time to read and give us encouragement. And thanks also to my editor Marie O'Regan for really helping to polish the pages of this book in the final stages.

And finally of course, to Riley, for having the wildest of imaginations, and for being my constant inspiration and motivation. You are an utter, creative genius.

From Riley...

Thank you Dad, for helping me write this book and for always supporting me. Thank you Mum for helping me and Dad with bringing Croc-Man and Wolf-Girl to life. Also thank you Eloise, you are the bomb!

Printed in Great Britain
by Amazon